Breakdown

Gateway, Volume 1

Imran Deen

Published by Imran Deen, 2024.

BREAKDOWN

First edition. April 1, 2024.

ISBN: 979-8224867141

Written by Imran Deen.

This book is dedicated to all te sword nerds who were born at
the wrong time.

It's also dedicated to Miss Bassano who made sure I never gave
up.

I can't forget Luna who was there from day one and Fairy who
stuck with me all the way.

Prologue

Tony walked straight to the counter and sat on a stool. The Jukebox in the corner played a soft Jazz. The lighting was dim and the bar almost empty. Of course, at 9 a.m., most people would be at work, not drinking. Only the wealthy, the lazy or those who have seen the other side would come here at this hour.

He lit a cigarette and signalled to the bartender. The Japanese bartender looked at him, looked at the sword attached to his waist and gave him a Blue Cherry Old Fashion, the drink most warriors preferred.

"Shanks. Long time no see," Tony said, offering him a cigarette.

The guy next to him was also drinking a beer. He was slightly larger than him. He was wearing a long black coat, like the ones Spanish Admirals wore, draped over him. Under that he was wearing plain black pants and a long-sleeved shirt, his right sleeve rolled up. His left sleeve was empty. He had an old scar over his left eye and a scruffy beard the same colour as his red hair.

"Tony," Shanks replied in a gravelly voice., accepting the cigarette.

The bartender quickly came over with an ashtray. A glowing red dot which emanated heat was fixed in the middle of the face.

"How long are you in town for?" Tony was always self-conscious around Shanks. His voice was notably higher.

"I don't know. Until I'm finished, I guess."

Tony raised his eyebrows questioningly. "Finished with what?" Tony asked.

"Some stuff," Shanks replied, infuriating Tony.

"Ah," Tony replied. He drank his Old Fashion, as good as ever. Shanks never gave much details and he wasn't trying to be infuriating. He was just one of those "super-cool" bad boy types, which got to him because Shanks was older than him by a good bit.

"Want to have a sparring match?" Shanks asked.

"Against you?"

"Yes, but also against someone else."

"Sure. Tell me when."

"I'll send details."

He had one arm but he was still one of the strongest men in the world. A fight against him was by and for an event many warriors only dreamed of.

Tony paid his tab and walked out of the bar, "I look forward to the match." He raised his hand, a white scar spanning the whole length of the back of his hand.

"You two do not get along, Mr Shanks?" the bartender asked.

Shanks let out a gravelly laugh. "Of course we do. He's my student after all."

"Oh! My apologize, Mr. Shanks. Here in Japan the relationship between teacher and student are very different, I would have never guessed!"

"Oh, the boy knows when to act as a student," Shanks said, running his fingers around the edge of the glass. Suddenly his voice turned very serious, as did his facial expression, and all the emotions in his eyes. "However, when you've faced life and death together many times, the relationship becomes far more than just teacher and student."

"I see. Well in that case, I think I understand," the bartender said.

Chapter 1

Jack the Ripper.

A name he detested but has stuck with him since the Magic Association's Adventurer's Test. The test involved surviving ten days inside a forested maze with every other participant who wished to become an adventurer that year. The goal was to get to the centre of the maze where flags equal to the number of participants could be found. The participant would then take a flag and return to the entrance of the maze, and would then be thus deemed a survivor.

Even though there was a ten-day time limit, Jack had finished the maze in three hours, killing everything in his path, and setting a record for the third fastest time to complete the test.

On the same day he passed he passed the test, eight others also passed, of which five people, including himself, set records as the fastest to complete the test.

A girl, Selena Conan whom passed by also killing everything in her path, and a guy a bit older than both of them who created an ice bridge to the centre and back. Together they set the second fastest time to finish the maze in two hours. The other two competitors were twin mages who both set a record for the fastest time to pass the test, finishing in under one hour.

Today Jack faced another test, his Special Grade Adventurer's Test. While both of the twin mages and Selena were not here today, Max was.

The Test was quite simple in theory, twenty-five participants were placed on an island in which there was a mountain in the middle. Adventurers were tasked with recovering one item scattered around the mountain and returning to the port. The first five adventures to return would be named as Special Grade Adventurers.

This left two choices, find an object and return to port quickly, or wait for another competitor to find an item and steal them, either by hurting them or killing them.

Jack had already managed to obtain his item, a small woollen doll which gave off no magical aura whatsoever but was emblazoned with the magic association's Mark. Not only that, he had gained an ally in Max, who had also obtained his item, a small wooden wheel which was extremely potent.

Jack and Max ran through the forest at top speed, reinforcing their body with mana as the made their way back to port.

"Someone's coming," said Max.

"I know," Jack said. "Run faster, I'll divert them."

"They're strong," Max said.

"Doesn't matter. I'm stronger," Jack said.

Max looked over at Jack for a second, seeing the determination on his face. Was it stupidity or did he believe he could fight them? Finally, Max took off into the forest, leaving Jack.

Jack stopped running and hid behind a tree. Soon the pursuer came into sight and passed Jack without noticing him. Jack drew his sword, a tachi he had acquired in Japan, and slashed it towards the man, coating his sword in wind magic. A slash of wind erupted from his sword following the curvature of his sword swing.

The slashed rushed towards the man who turned, shocked that he couldn't sense Jack. Jack's attack slashed the man's shoulder, cutting him and spraying blood everywhere.

"Go join the Thieves' Guild, scumbag," Jack said, walking towards the man.

The man let out a whimper as blood spread across his body. Jack held out his hand and started casting healing magic over him, stopping the bleeding. "You aren't even worth killing." He reached down and pulled a glass bottle from the man's pocket, and smashing it on the ground between his legs.

Green dust spread across the ground, forming the shape of a pentagram enclosed within two circles, which encapsulated a row of runes and a star in the middle. The green circle glowed bright red and the man disappeared, leaving a black burn on the ground in the form of the symbol.

The mana in the area became unstable as the mana in the area rushed to fill the vacuum that was created at an uneven and uncontrolled rate.

"Jack!" Max called out, rushing towards him. His voice was somehow loud and soft at the same time. His tall muscular frame came lumbering towards Jack. "You ok?"

"Yes of course I am," Jack replied, looking up at Max who was a foot taller than him and almost double his width. Jack raised his hand in front of him and cast a wind detection spell throughout the area surrounding them.

A light breeze passed through the trees and marked the location of every leaf, rock, twig and living being that it touched.

"We're being surrounded," Jack said to Max. "There are chimeras on our north, northeast and northwest sides. There're a couple magic ants who just turned and are marching towards us from the south, southeast and west. And finally, there are two hydrae coming from the southwest."

"Which leaves only the East for us to go."

"No. Bad call," Jack stated. "We have to go Southeast to get back to the port which is directly in front of us."

"Where the magic ants are."

"Yes."

"Ok I can fight ants."

"Me to. We're going Northeast," Jack said.

"What? Port is Southeast. We'll be going in the different direction!"

"Correct. However, there is a clearing northeast of here. If we hurry, we can get to it and change direction from there, circling around any magic creatures, but we have to hurry."

"Understood," Max said. "You're right. But if we do encounter any monsters, we run, not fight, ok?"

"Agreed," Jack said, nodding his head.

They both took off running, reinforcing their leg muscles with mana. They zipped through the forest, which was easy since the trees grew far apart and many of the roots were down trodden from years of being walked on by magical creatures many times the size of humans.

Jack ran in front of Max, turning and twisting so that they could get to the clearing in the fastest way possible. The first thing they noticed was the smell; extremely strong sulphur, mixed with the taste of salt. The air also got noticeably hotter the closer they got.

Finally, the broke through the trees and entered the clearing. The entire ground was black and radiated heat. There were a few soft spots with a black gooey liquid and small puddles of water mixed with oil and sulphur around them. A few lone trees sprouted around the area, the wood a dark colour, but their leaves deep shades of blue and red.

"A Pitch Lake," Max said in awe.

"Yeah. It's a wonder that no one has tried harvesting it yet," Jack said.

"It is indeed."

"C'mon," Jack said, running on the edge of the lake. He could feel his foot sinking into the soft ground as he ran, both making the run easier by absorbing the shock and quieting the run. Max ran close behind him.

"Slow down Jack," Max panted from behind him.

Jack turned to see Max beaded with sweat. He didn't realise how hot the area was since he could control his own body temperature. Suddenly stopping also made him realise how much his muscles ached. He and Max had been running from the centre of the island for at least an hour non-stop. Reinforcing their body with mana helped provide support to their body but didn't stop it from experiencing the intense physical burnout.

"Ok. Take a break," Jack said.

"Thanks," Max said, taking a drink from the water skin he carried. Jack also took his out and took a long drink.

He then raised his hand again and started whispering a spell under his breath, "Take the form of a Zephyr and show me what surrounds me." The same gentle wind blew across the area with Jack at the centre, telling him the position of everything close by.

"Jack?" asked Max.

"We're in the clear. But not too far from here there's another participant with two hydrae heading to them. The person is currently fighting a couple ants."

"Let's go help them," Max said indignantly.

"I thought you'd say that," Jack said grimly. "It's a bit out of our way.

"Do you think the person will be ok alone?" Max asked.

"No."

"Then there's nothing to think about."

"We only have three hours left to get to the meeting point."

"So?"

Jack thought about it for a while. Not too far from where the hydrae were also a group of ants and possibly some beetles but he wasn't entirely sure. Most likely the bugs were fighting amongst themselves but he couldn't be sure. Was it worth the risk?

"If you want to go then go ahead."

A look crossed Max's face. Jack wondered if he'd punch him. "Show me the way," Max said finally through gritted teeth.

Jack nodded his head. He turned away from Max and walked to the closest tree. He plucked several leaves and then reached in his pocket for his lighter. He set the leaves on the ground and lit them on fighter. "Needle, Cardinal. North Star. Poles. Show the way I am thinking of,"

Jack chanted, thinking of the person in his mind. The smoke rose into the air and moved in the direction of the person.

Max looked at Jack who motioned to follow the smoke. Max nodded and ran off; all his tiredness now forgotten

Chapter 2

Max couldn't believe Jack. A person was in danger but all he cared about was the stupid test. Max followed where the smoke carried him, careful not to break the thread. Soon he could hear loud crashing in front of him. He walked towards the sound, drawing his dagger from his belt. The blade was serpentine built and it was bright blue and shining. Jack looked at the hilt and saw that it was pure bronze, then at the pommel and saw that it was pure silver. The stone was the entire blue blade.

Twigs crushed underfoot as Max got closer to the fight. Soon he was in range to sense the group of living creatures fighting in the forest. Max took a deep breath and walked forwards faster.

Soon he was in sight and saw a young woman with a sword drawn in front of her with a group of beetles almost double her height surrounding her.

The young lady was about four- and three-quarter feet tall, with long blonde hair and startlingly blue eyes. The blade she held in front of her was covered in blood but luckily it appeared she wasn't hurt. There were around three beetles lying dead in the area, but around five were surrounding her. There was just barely enough room to swing her sword as it was.

After assessing the situation, Max decided on what he was going to do. A swift attack to kill all the beetles at once. He took a deep breath, exhaling through his mouth, readying himself.

He bent down and pressed the tip of the dagger into the ground. "Break through the ground and pierce my enemies." He poured his mana into his blade, focusing on what he wanted to happen.

From the tip of his dagger the ground suddenly frozen over and then was covered in a layer of ice. Great icicles broke through the ground below the beetles. Max watched with triumph as the icicles hit the underbelly of the beetles, but his spirit was immediately crushed when the icicles were crushed against the tough exoskeleton of the beetles.

He steeled himself, refocusing his mana, "Bind my enemy. Let them neither escape nor give them room to attack."

Immediately the ice expanded around the beetles and froze them in place.

Max panted from the effort he had exerted. At least he was no longer melting in the heat.

He looked up at the woman, whom had her sword raised in Max's direction and a scared look in her eyes.

Max got up off the ground and walked slowly towards the woman with both his hands raised in a gesture of surrender. "I came to help you," he said, hoping to calm the woman.

"How do I know that?" the woman asked in a high-pitched voice.

"I have no reason to attack you," Max said. "I have already completed the challenge."

"If you already completed the challenge, why would you come to help me?" the woman asked sceptically.

"Because, you're in danger," Max said.

"Yeah, no kidding," the woman said, referring to the beetles but not looking away for even a second.

"There are two hydrae headed here," Max said.

The woman's sword wavered for a second, but she looked like she was reconsidering. She could sense the artifact in Max's pocket so there was no chance he was here to steal hers.

"Alright," the woman said, lowering her sword. "I'm Jessica."

"Ok Jessica. I'm Max."

Jessica nodded, wiping blood from her face. She really was quite beautiful.

She sheathed her sword and raised her hands in front of her, he palms facing towards her body. She whispered something and all of the blood and dirt on her collected in a small ball in her hand, which she threw aside.

"So, hydrae?" she asked.

"Yes," Max said. She really was quite beautiful. "Two of them."

Jessica nodded. "Ok then. I'll take your word for it. I'm not much of a sensor. Which direction are they coming from?"

"Oh, um." Max laughed nervously. "I don't actually know. Someone I was with discovered them, but we split up not too far from here."

Jessica gave Max a look that he couldn't quite pin down, like a mix of anger and disbelief at his stupidity. "So, we can't run because we don't know which way to go?"

"Um, yeah, I guess."

"What about the direction you came from?"

"I don't think that's a good idea. A group of monsters are collecting there."

Jessica took a deep breath and sighed. "Ok fine, I guess we fight."

Max nodded.

"Freeze the ground around us. The ice was you right?"

"Yes, it was."

"Good. Freeze the ground." She pressed her hands together and started muttering under her breath. The air around them started shimmering. Max plunged the tip of his dagger into the ground again, speaking his chant and calling ice to freeze the area around them.

Jessica opened her eyes. "Now we wait," she said.

Five minutes later they sensed mana flaring west of their position then everything went still. Two minutes after that, they felt the earth around them tremble.

Finally, a minute after the earth stopped shaking a hydra appeared before them. This one only had three heads. Jessica drew her sword and

Max his dagger and both waited until it noticed them. They didn't need to wait long.

"Target the heart," Jessica said, raising her sword and bringing it down in an arc in front of her. Mana radiated from the blade, forming a long red arc that rushed towards the hydra, severing one of its head off.

The head fell to the ground and turned to ash. The neck started splitting in two along its length until there were two fully formed necks. Next the head started reforming. The bones were the first to grow back, with tendons and ligaments following, connecting the bones. Organs and skin started growing at the same time, and for a point the two heads looked naked and vulnerable, but then bright green and deep scales started forming to match the body. Finally, the red eyes and the black teeth were borne. The entire process took less than five seconds to take place.

The hydra looked directly at Jessica and Max and let out four blood curling roars at once. It rushed at them, its stubby legs slipping on the ice in front of them. The hydra fell over, it's tail thrashing and his legs kicking the air.

"Scatter," Jessica said calmly.

Max nodded and the two of the took off running in the different direction. The hydra got back on his feet and rushed at Max. Jessica stopped and turned, raising her sword and once again slashed it in an arc in the direction of the hydra. This time the arc cut deep into the hydra, splitting it in half, and splitting the heart, killing it instantly.

Max turned and headed back towards Jessica, side stepping the Hydra corpse. Before they could reunite another hydra appeared. This one had eight heads and was almost double the size. Seeing its fallen comrade, it let out an eight-way roar. Jessica and Max stopped in place. Max raised his dagger in front of him and Jessica raised her sword, both of them extremely scared of what would happen next.

Suddenly the ground shook, and a projectile came shooting out of the woods behind them. In a second the hydra was set aflame. It let out a couple desperate roars.

"Run," said Jessica.

"Run," Max agreed.

They both took off, not concerned with the direction they were going, as long as it was away from the burning hydra.

Soon they came to a clearing. Several dead bugs lay scattered around the area and blood covered everything they looked. Jessica and Max stopped to take in the scene, their weapons at the ready.

They were both shaking in their shoes. Usually when something died, they gave off copious amounts of mana, but this time there was nothing.

"Let's go," Jessica said.

They both ran off from the terrible scene.

An hour later they arrived at the port, the meeting point to show they'd achieved their task. They presented their artifacts to the examiners.

"Is Jack back yet?" Max asked the proctor who was collecting the items.

"No. He hasn't returned yet," the proctor said.

Chapter 3

Jack's tachi was utterly destroyed in the last test. That's why he was here, in the swords district of Japan where he could have a new sword made. Japanese swords were special as the metal used was the finest grade in the world and the swordsmiths were unrivalled. Their traditional forging techniques provided blades that even incompetent men could use. This was also one of the only places in the world where a person was freely allowed to roam with their weapon, albeit with a license.

He walked down the Sakura lined road and didn't even glance at the trees. Carrying the damaged sword made Jack feel irritable and angry. Each sword had its own soul. That is the first principle that each swordsman was taught. A sword can strongly affect a person's mood and feelings. Some say it brings confidence or foolhardiness. Others say that the feelings are brought about when the sword projects its own feelings and memories onto the swordsman. Swordsmen are taught that each sword should be treated like the carrier's spouse. This sword was asking to be divorced. He couldn't enjoy the beautiful day nor the scenery. And instead of happy victories, this sword projected only negativity.

Jack arrived at the swordsmith's shop he had been seeking. This particular swordsmith, Chimoto Tsumari, used tool steel in his work. Tool steel was frowned upon in the Japanese sword making community, however, the swords themselves were stronger and more resilient. It didn't dull as fast and was less prone to cracks. There were no rules against using tool steel swords in the fighting community either but it was also frowned upon as a tool steel sword broke traditional sword easily. It goes without saying that breaking a sword was taboo with the whole "Your sword is your spouse" principle.

Jack looked around the shop. Several swords were on display along the walls with quite pricey numbers underneath them. On the right were less expensive swords which Jack could see were lower quality. There were also loose blades, scabbards, that he assumed were collector's souvenirs, and guards that could be fitted to different swords.

Jack looked closely at the individual blades. On the tang he saw inscriptions in Japanese characters. These inscriptions, he knew, were the author's signature and general information about the swords. Some swordsmiths only inlaid their initials or name on blades but other information that could be present on swords include the material, date of production, smithing techniques and the like. The more information on a blade the more easily the sword could be traced and value given.

On closer inspection he realized the swords had no hamon. Hamons were the result of softer steels being inlaid on top of harder steels. The blade, once finished, was given an acid bath and the softer steel would become darker based on a chemical reaction called etching. Of course, most Japanese swords had a hamon but it is not a requirement as the acid bath was purely aesthetic. However, he knew that tool steel swords had no hamons as there were no hard or soft steel, only a processed alloy made from specific metals in specific amounts.

To the left of the display cabinet a sword tinged with a bluish hue caught his eye.

A little Japanese woman emerged from a door behind the counter while he was inspecting the blade. He didn't notice her until she spoke. "How can I help you, young man?"

This startled Jack. He wasn't supposed to be startled. He was supposed to be highly trained to be aware of his surroundings at all times, prepared for a fight at a moment's notice. He blamed the sword. He was sure that the sword was harbouring ill feelings towards him for replacing it. He removed the sword and scabbard and placed it on the counter.

"I need a replacement," he said. "My name is Jack Drake. I called 2 weeks ago and asked to meet Mr. Chimoto about making me three standard sized katanas."

"Yes. I am well aware of who you are, Mr. Jack the Ripper. And it is Ms. Chimoto. That would be me you talked to over the telephone," the woman- Ms Chimoto- replied.

Jack was surprised. He expected Chimoto to be a he; a large, muscular he. However, looking at the woman he realized, under the slightly loose clothes she was wearing, she was fairly muscular and not out of shape. Her hands were crossed behind her back but he knew, now, that those hands would be slightly pink or have minor burns on them from working the hot metal. "My apologies Ms. Chimoto. Your English is very good. But would you please not call me Jack the Ripper. Drake should do fine, or Jack if you prefer."

"Drake then."

"Yes," Chimoto made Jack nervous. She was not intimidated by him and she was entirely calm. "Well...yes. I've come to acquire two new swords, full length tachis, specially made."

"Right this way young man." Chimoto turned and walked back through the door, leading the way through another room and through another door for Jack.

Jack walked into a workshop where he saw different tools like power hammers and belt sanders along with the traditional anvils and hammers. The differences in sound between the workshop and the store was astounding as he realized the workshop was isolated to not disturb the customers. Jack looked around in awe but followed closely behind Chimoto. She was not the type to wait for him but she was the type to scold him for falling behind.

Jack followed as Chimoto turned a corner and entered another room, this one featuring a table and couch, several chairs and a few tools he couldn't identify. Chimoto took out a tea set and poured hot green tea into a traditional tea bowl for Jack.

"Ok Drake. What type of swords are you looking for?" Chimoto asked, wasting no time.

Jack looked up from observing his tea bowl. Japanese tea bowls always featured different and unique patterns and designs. This lady wasted no time though. It was all business for her.

"I want the highest-grade tool steel-" Jack began.

"Yes yes," Chimoto interrupted him. "No one comes here looking for a low quality tamahagane sword." She was referring to the traditional and highly renowned Japanese jewel steel that was the basis for most Japanese swords.

"Right," Jack said, clearing his throat. "I want two full length tachis, steel fittings and a bronze mekugi pin."

"Ok," Chimoto said, taking a note on a pad Jack didn't notice earlier. "Why don't you want brass fittings?"

"Steel fittings are better," Jack replies. "Oh, and I want all the fittings to be painted black."

Chimoto looked at him, but only made a note. "And the reason for the Mekugi pins?"

Jack knew traditional mekugi pins were made of bamboo. Some swordsmiths, lesser swordsmiths, used brass but he wanted bronze. "Call it preference. It's a tool steel blade. A wooden Mekugi pin will shatter."

"Ok," Chimoto said. "What else?"

"The handle must be relatively thin. Black ito wrap over a red samegawa."

Chimoto looked at him. "I do not die my Ray Skin."

"I don't want Ray Skin. I want red silk wrapped with black leather."

Chimoto pursed her lips and made a note. "Will that be all?"

"No," Jack replied. "Sharpen and polish the blades by hand."

Chimoto raised her eyebrows at him. "Very well."

Jack looked at her. Chimoto looked back, in the eye.

"It will cost you around $300 000 USD each."

"Ok," Jack replied.

"It will take around 3 months," Chimoto continued.

"Can't I have it before?" Jack asked.

"No," Chimoto said. "You want each blade hand sharpened. Tool steel is not easy to sharpen."

"Very well," Jack said.

"I need half now and half when you collect the swords," Chimoto said. Jack withdrew $500 000 USD from his inside jacket pocket in 10 000 Yen notes. "Here is $500 000. I'll settle the account on completion."

"Very well," Chimoto replied. "I need you to sign a document stating that you waive this money from failure to collect the swords. You also waive the right to demand the swords after 6 months of being contacted about the completion of the swords and failure to collect unless you make other arrangements to collect."

"Very well," Jack replied.

"Good. I'll get the documents ready. Please wait here and help yourself to some tea."

Chimoto got up and took her notepad and the money back into the workshop and headed to, what he presumed, was her office.

He disliked the old hag. Everyone knew sword makers were inferior, tools that made tools. They served no real purpose, had no real effect on the world. They served to obey the swordsmen. But the hag with her airs about her thinking she was superior to him. She thought she could intimidate him. She demanded money like he was some pauper and spoke to him like he was a child, calling him Jack the Ripper. If he knew any other swordsmith who used tool steel he would have left her right there, but no, he had no choice.

He sat there fuming to himself, refusing to drink the tea.

***

"I do not like this one," Chimoto said, entering her office.

Shanks was sitting in there on a stool, this time shedding his coat and with a sword on the back of his belt, the handle facing to the right. This sword was Western style featuring a hand guard. It was made specifically for him by Chimoto to use with his one arm. The handguard ensured that the sword would not slip out. Everything else about the sword was Japanese style, with a long handle and a single beveled edge. This sword was special as it was one of few of Chimoto's swords made of Tamahagane. Furthermore, it was hand forged and hand sharpened, with over 2000 layers of the high-grade metal, and of course cursed.

Shanks smiled and said nothing.

"He's pompous and rude," Chimoto continued. "No respect for us swordsmiths. He's one of those swordsmen who think swordsmiths are nothing."

"Yes yes," Shanks said. "But remember, I was like that once too."

"No, you weren't," Chimoto said. "You knew how to respect someone. He's a horrible little man."

Shanks smiled and said nothing.

Chimoto looked at him with disapproval. "I don't know if I'll take the commission."

Shanks chuckled. "Take it."

Chimoto looked at him. "Why? He's a brat. I don't want him."

Shanks looked at her with a straight face. "Take it."

"Why should I?"

"He has potential."

"Three words don't constitute an explanation-," Chimoto started.

"He has a certain skill that could come in quite handy in the future," Shanks cut her off.

Chimoto looked slightly offended, "I beg your pardon?"

Shanks smiled a little but kept with his serious tone, "There are certain things going on in the world right now, and he has potential to play a major role in it."

"So, he's special?"

"No. No, not at all. He's an ordinary magic swordsman but with a few skills he's developed that could prove useful."

"What things are happening?"

"That I cannot disclose at this moment, but you know you'll find out when the time is right."

"I see. Very well then."

"You'll take it? Excellent," he got up from his seat and started heading for the door. "I'll be seeing you around Tsumari."

Chimoto let out a sigh. "Goodbye-"

The closing door cut her off. Shanks had already left.

Chapter 4

After finishing all the paperwork, Chimoto accompanied Jack to the front of the building into the store area.

"Thank you for doing business with us Drake. I hope you come again," Chimoto was saying. He was still a client, no matter how much he disliked him.

"Wait," Jack said. "That." and he pointed to his old sword, "Get rid of it."

"I beg your pardon?" Chimoto was mollified. Get rid of the sword? Was he out of his mind?

"Get rid of it. Do what you want. It's a good make but it's damaged. I don't know what to do with it but I don't want it. Keep it or discard it or give it back to the creator. I don't care."

Chimoto looked horrified at these words. This boy.

"Also. I need a sword. That one," Jack said, indicating a sword hung on the wall with a black and blue scabbard and a black ito wrap over ray skin. "I want that one."

Chimoto looked at him and pursed her lips. "Very well."

She took a key from around her neck and unlocked the glass wall between them and the sword. The wall was almost invisible, if not for the translucent locks. It was really well crafted. It had thick glasses forming a divider between the customers and the swords, but it was highly polished and the lighting was ingenuous so that without close inspection, the wall was practically invisible. Even the locks were translucent and with the lightings you totally missed it. When the door opened, it slid neatly into the next door, almost hovering, so that it was once again invisible.

Chimoto handed the sword to Jack. Jack looked it up and down. Then smelt it. This sword was different. The other swords were all tool steel.

This sword was pure iron and dyed a deep blue. It had no patterns in the blade, a sign that there were no impurities or carbon in the bade. It was without doubt the only unique sword in the showroom. On the flat side of the blade was "◇◇". This Kanji, he knew, meant protection. "I'll take it," Jack said.

Chimoto walked back to the register. She cashed the sword based on the price tag under the sword, for which Jack paid cash for. Then she took out two certificates, one of authentication showing that she made the sword and giving details of the sword. The second was an affidavit of sorts, saying that although she sold the weapon, she is not responsible for anything done with the sword. Jack signed it with a smile on his face. This entire process happened without a word. She wrapped the sword in a carrying cloth and escorted him to the door. "Please come back soon," Chimoto said, bowing as is custom in Japan. Jack left without a word, holding his sword.

"Kimyōna kodomo wa nandesuka," she said- What a weird kid.

***

Jack walked down the street happily with his new sword. He made his way to the bullet trains where he went to his hotel room. Extraordinarily pleased with himself, he took off his shirt and poured himself a drink from the small bar provided to him. He looked out at Tokyo from his 24th floor hotel room. The room itself wasn't luxurious but at the same time it wasn't exactly uncomfortable. He had a large bed with nightstands on either side, his own bathroom and a small bar, and other smaller amenities. He also had a spectacular view of the city from his window.

Just then he heard a knock at his door. "Just a second," he called out. It wouldn't do to receive persons in his undershirt. He pulled on a sweater and went to open the door. Halfway there he stopped and turned around. He unfurled the wrappings of his sword and took it out of the carrying cloth Ms Chimoto put it in. He left the sword close to the door on the dressing table which was midway between the door and the far side of the room. He could easily grab the sword if need be. He went back to the door and opened it slowly. There was no peephole to look through.

Jack opened the door slowly and was shocked. In the doorway stood Shanks. He immediately opened the door all the way and allowed him inside.

"Mr Shanks," Jack began. "What are you doing here?" Jack was a bit flustered.

"I'm here to give you an assignment," Shanks said. Then stopped. He looked on the dresser at the katana lying there. "Midway between the door and the far wall. Easily retrievable. Smart."

He walked up to the katana and looked over it without touching it. "Why is it here?"

"I bought it today from Ms-"

"Chimoto. I know. It was there today."

Jack raised his eyebrows, cleared his throat and replied, "Yeah. I needed a sword because mine is broken."

"Yes yes, I know all about your broken sword. I saw the test. Why'd you buy it?"

"Well, it's a nice sword and-" Jack began.

"Don't lie to me," Shanks cut across him. "There are many words to describe this sword. Nice is not one." Jack swallowed. "This sword is cursed. You know that right? Right?" Jack nodded. Shanks looked him up and down then took a seat on one of three chairs that came with the room.

"Would you like anything to drink?" Jack asked, relieved that Shanks dropped the topic.

"No," Shanks replied. He then reached into his coat, which he wore this time instead of draping it around himself, and pulled out a folder, holding it out for Jack. Jack took it and sat on the chair opposite Shanks. He laid it out on the bar that separated them and started reading. He then picked up his glass and took a drink, finishing the half glass that remained in one swallow.

He looked at Shanks, his face somewhat pale. "How long 'til it happens?" He forgot to speak formally, instead lapsing back into his accent that was no help at all in identifying where he came from, as constant travel had butchered any individuality in his voice.

"Long enough for you to get your swords and finish mastering your two-sword style," Shanks replied.

"I'm not learning a two-sword style," Jack replied. "I'm creating a three-sword style."

"What?" Shanks looked at him incredulously. As serious as the matter was, the absurdity that just left Jack's mouth would make any competent swordsman lose their train of thought. "How, exactly, does a three-sword style make sense?"

"It's my own creation. I'll make it work," Jack replied defensively.

"Whatever," Shanks said. "Do whatever stupidity you like. But prepare for that. Practically."

"Yes, sir."

"Good." Shanks got up, ready to leave.

"That's it?" asked Jack.

"Yup," Shanks replied. He walked to the door.

"But I have questions," Jack said.

"Too bad kid. Everything we know is in that file."

"It's two freaking pages."

"And that's everything we know." Shanks stepped out and closed the door. Jack was stunned.

Chapter 5

Jack entered the Grand Hall in Greece at two thirty in the morning of the 20th of December. The day was warm and sunny, the heat beating down on Jack's neck. His black long sleeve shirt was rolled up to the elbows, his shirt untucked and his hair messy. His new sword, which he called Hogo for the Kanji letter on it, was on his belt. His black pants were tucked into his leather boots that stopped just before his knees. He wore leather jewellery and beads, no metal. He also had a few bandages wrapped around his arm where he had gotten nicked while practicing with his sword. It was indeed cursed, but that was fixed with a bit of force. Control, he knew, was always needed on a sword. Cursed or not, just determined how much stricter he needed to be.

Generally speaking, when entering the Grand Hall, people tend to wear formal clothes to be respectful. But since he was summoned here two weeks ago with a two-page document, one of the pages saying war was upon them and the other being the summons itself, he decided he should be prepared to fight at any time.

Jack strode down the Grand Hall into corridor 8. The Grand Hall itself was a "ruin", except it wasn't exactly a ruin. The place was magically preserved so that it was more than just usable, it was a stronghold. The Council used this as their base of operations since the early 11th Century after the fall of the magic community in China during the time of the Song Dynasty. Two other bases on the same level existed in Europe, established during the High Middle Ages when Dragon hunting was extremely popular, and Haiti, where it survived near extinction conditions but now flourish as a counter culture. Finally, there was the main headquarters in Trinidad, which was a meeting point of sorts that hosted cultures originating in India, Europe, Africa and many other parts of the world. He had yet to see the Trinidad Headquarters where the council of 10 was hosted but he had heard that the country held many wonders because of the sheer number of cohabitating cultures trading their secrets.

At the centre of each hall held a three-dimensional representation of the 9 realms magically suspended on a pedestal. At the centre stood a spherical image with three mountains and linked all the other spheres. The special thing about this sphere was that it was inverted, flat with the sphere being an invisible force with the same presence as Earth's atmosphere. The sphere was circum-divided, with the top mirroring the bottom. This flat representation gained many names throughout the years with Eden being the most common.

On the west stood the earth, Man's land.

At the East stood Arthe, The Land of Fae. A small bridge connected Arthe and Earth.

On the North stood Rathe, the land of Elves. A small bridge also connected Earth and Rathe.

On the East stood Vearth, the land of Dwarves. This was the only land with no connections to any of the other realms.

On the highest peak of the three mountains, a gateway was present, leading to Olympus, home of Titans.

Going further upwards from Olympus stood Heaven, land of Angels.

Mirrored on the highest peak of the three mountains of the bottom side of the Connecting World a gateway ran, connecting Erebos, the land of Demons. Erebos was connected to Earth and no other realms. This gave rise to the Greek legends of the Underworld.

Below Erebos, Tartarus was connected, home of Devils.

There was one other realm, not connected to any of the others nor the Connecting World. No one lived there and it had yet to be named.

A man stood outside a tinted conference room, seemingly waiting on him.

Why was he waiting on him? Why are they meeting in a conference room? How many members are going to be present to explain a mission to him? Should he have worn something better if he was meeting so many people?

"Mr Jack Drake?" the man asked him. The man was wearing all black, carried no visible weapons and had the look of a soldier.

"Yeah," Jack said. He didn't need to be formal with a mere soldier. He probably only did grunt work anyway. He didn't even have a weapon.

"Your meeting will take place here Mr Drake," he said, opening the door.

"Thanks," Jack said.

Jack walked in and, to his surprise, ten people were inside. They were seated around a long black table that could hold twenty-one persons. The table was arranged as a king's would be, with one chair at the head of the table and an equal number on both sides. They were grouped together with a few seats in between themselves.

One looked like a male official. He was wearing a dark suit with a coat draped over his shoulders. The coat was white. He recognised the two mages who sat beside him as the who set the record for the fastest times to complete the Magic Association Test, Micheal and Michelle They had large mana pools that he could sense. They carried no weapons but the clothes they wore looked all natural, probably high-quality cotton. The clothes themselves were formal traditional clothing- the country beyond him. The scary part was that he couldn't tell if they were male or female. The clothes were similar for both, both loose fitting. Their hair was long and he couldn't see their hands. They both looked extremely similar as well. Neither feminine nor masculine. It was mildly off-putting.

Four other men sat opposite these three, all in black and white suits. Three had swords accompanying them and one had a naginata. Two seats next to them were empty and then one woman occupied the next in line, Selena. She wore a white jacket and a black leather pants. Her ears glinted with piercings and her red hair was braided with several metal beads. She had a European straight sabre next to her. These five persons had significant mana pools; that is, it was above civilians but it was not cause for concern.

The ninth person intrigued him. His mana pool was quite dense. He sat on the furthest side of the table, to the left of the head. His mana wastage was quite low and the overall feel was that of a well sharpened blade. He was obviously quite skilled in his practices. Jack was unsure whether he was a swordsman or a mage. He wouldn't have been surprised if either was the case. He wore a full black suit, including an expensive looking black shirt.

The person sitting at the head was quite intimidating but not in an oppressive way. He was large and well built, which was saying a lot as everyone here was, for the most part, in top shape. He wore a white suit with a black shirt, and had a white coat over it. His hair was grey and neatly groomed, and he had a full grey beard. He had no visible weapons with him but he had no doubt he could do considerable damage without it.

"Jack the Ripper," he said in a voice like a bull. But still, it wasn't loud or dismissive or even actively scary. Not even authoritative. It was devoid of emotion but at the same time it evoked respect and submission. This intrigued him beyond anything. The man was an anomaly. "Come. Take a seat to my right. We are waiting until the other eleven join us."

Jack took his appointed seat without a word. He saw that a file was placed in front of him, considerably thicker than two pages.

"Go on and read," the bull voiced man said. "I'm sure you have many questions and want details as soon as possible."

Jack opened the file and started reading. The file had considerably more details and explained the atmosphere in the room. Everyone was silent and not talking to each other. Jack was shaken to his core by what he was reading. Page after page he turned, taking in the words on them, becoming more and more shocked by what he was reading.

Chapter 6

Well, it definitely was a world ending threat.

Several millennia ago, during the great age of Sorcery, Mages of different races came together and performed feats of magic never before seen, creating the World End Gates. These Gates stood at the entrance of each World's bridge into Eden.

These Gates were necessary for two reasons. The first was that it allowed the native species of each World to control who comes in and out of their world, like an interworld airport. The second, more important reason, was to stop creatures from crossing over into other worlds.

Of course, Pathways would sometimes naturally form, linking two worlds together. This happened during Earth's Dark and Middle Ages when dragons started entering the World causing severe consequences. This time was dubbed "the Great Beast Wars" in recent times and signified Man's determination to regulate movement in and out of their world.

Now that the Gates were breaking down, Pathways were now stating to pop up all over the worlds and Eden, causing magical beasts to start crossing over unrestricted. This caused major disasters, especially when Titanic beasts started rampaging. The Magic Association and the Earth Magic Council were hard pressed to contain the situation as they appeared.

The second, more major problem appeared when the Demon Race started to invade Eden. In the midst of the natural Pathways popping up in the world, the Demon Race launched a full-scale invasion to take Eden, migrating millions of species of animals and demons. This led the

Inter-World Magic Coalition to come to a decision to mount defences at the head of their Gateways to prevent an invasion into their world.

Of course, Earth had it a lot tougher than any other, as there was a direct Pathway between Erebos, the Demon World, and Earth. This meant that Earth had to have a constant guard in the event that the Demon Race decided Earth was a good target.

Luckily, Earth was also connected to Arthe, the world of Fae, and Rathe, the world of Elves. This Led the Inter-World Magic Coalition to realise that an invasion of Earth would mean an invasion of every world. Therefore, Earth should expect reinforcements from both Arthe and Rathe.

These sentries were a temporary though, and this is where Jack came in. Jack needed to go to Arthe to retrieve a specific item from there that would hopefully help restore the Gates and contain the Pathways.

Meanwhile, Earth, Arthe, Rathe and Vearth would lead troops to reclaim Eden. Leading the Human race into battle was the "chosen one", a man born with the highest mana reserves recorded in history and could perform feats that seemed impossible, even among the extraordinary.

Jack would have been able to complete this task in a matter of days. But he had a team. To Jack, teams always slowed him down. Because he had to watch another person's back, he was unable to fight to his fullest. Nor was he able to use the full extent of his power because he would injure his team.

But according to the council, Jack would be unable to complete the quest on his own.

He had a team of five. The first two members were Selena and Max. Jack was appointed leader; a decision contested by Max. Max cited the fact that Jack refused to help Jessica as a reason why he was unfit to lead. After some debate, it was decided that the decision would remain unchanged. The other two members were Michelle and Micheal, both of whom he'd met before, neither of whom he'd had the opportunity to work with.

Overall, Jack was satisfied with this line-up, three S-Ranked Members of the Magic Association, although he still though he could achieve his goal without them.

***

For three months, Jack and his team were fighting off Magical beasts that invaded Earth. They had to wait for winter to finish before they could leave since the Magic Association felt the need to have as many S-Ranked fighters on hand until Spring, since Winter was when Demons were naturally at their strongest, and spring was when Humans were at their strongest.

At the start of spring, Jack collected his new swords from Chimoto and him and his team gathered at the Arthe-Earth Gateway.

"Ok Jack," a nondescript officer of the council said. He wore a high ranked uniform, and had neither given his name nor had Jack asked for it. From a conversation between him and another officer, Jack had gathered that the officer was a Sergeant. "The gateway is a bit unstable. The way these Gateways were created was by magic millions of years ago when magic was much less refined compared to now. I advise you to not spend long in there."

"Understood, Sergeant," Jack replied. "What happens if we do spend a long time there?"

"Let's just say," Sergeant replied, a grim look in his eyes, "It won't be pretty. Much stronger beings have tried going through and they barely survived. I wish you luck."

"Thank you, Sergeant. We'll be on our way now. Much luck to you on this side," Jack said, saluting the officer.

"Ok listen up," Jack said to his team, who were observing the exchange between Sergeant and Jack, "You all heard the man. No standing around staring. Quick movement. Understood?"

"Yessir," they all replied in unison.

"Micheal. Michelle. Guard our backs. There's no telling what could be in there. If danger comes knocking, it's your job to stop it with magic."

"Yessir," they replied.

"Selena. Max. I'm sure I don't need to tell you this but keep your defences up until we know what's back there. This means full mana skin," Jack commanded.

"Yessir," they replied.

Jack looked at his team. Although they had spent three months fighting together, practicing moves and finding their balance, it was clear that they were still nervous and unable to stand together as one.

"And guys. Remember. We have each other's back. Anything that presents itself in there, we can counter it. We're the best of the best. The strongest ones out there. And remember, the Council trusts us. Out of millions of swordsmen and mages, the Council trusts us to carry out this mission. We can do this." This feeble attempt at a speech seemed to rally them a little as a little bit of hope entered back into their eyes.

"Yessir," Selena said, her mouth forming a small half smile.

"Good. Let's go," Jack said. "I'll be going first."

With that, Jack walked through the gateway. Following him was Max, then the twins entered together, holding hands. Finally, Selena brought up the rear.

***

After entering the Gateway, Jack fell.

Under him was no solid ground. He decided to use a spell to make him fly. Holding out his right hand, Jack started condensing mana and focusing on what he wanted. He noticed, however, that collecting mana was extremely difficult. *He can't use magic in a Gateway. Not on his own. Maybe....*

Next Jack tried a trick he learned while practicing to fly. He held out his right hand once again, and with his left hand he held the pendant around his throat. The pendant, as far as he knew, was jade, but he also knew that there were magical properties that came with it. Through trial and error, he found that when using wind spells, the Jade exuded magic and boosted his magical power in the spell. This was a secret he didn't tell any of the others as he was unsure what they would think, especially since he didn't remember where he got the pendant from. He gathered up his mana, now boosted by the pendant, and unleashed a burst of wind beneath him, stopping him in midair.

He wasn't flying, but he wasn't falling either, which was a good thing. Looking down, Jack risked focusing some of his mana into his eyes, trying to see if there was a bottom. A way down, probably two miles or so, Jack saw what looked like solid land where he could walk. He decreased the amount of mana in his wind spell and stopped the mana flow to his eyes, giving him a controlled descent to the ground. Upon landing, he killed his spell and refocused the mana into his eyes, looking for his team mates. Ahead, he saw that the twin mages were holding on to Max and Selena as they held their staffs upwards casting a spell to safely land them on the ground.

Jack shot off a simple burst of mana like a flare that would signal to them where he was. After five minutes he shot another. After the flare, his vision soon became blurred. He was running low on mana. He decided that his team would make it on the ground and find him. Even without the flares, he was sure that Micheal would track him easily. He was good at that sort of thing. He deactivated his Mana Sight and instead worked on keeping his mana skin intact. This was a fruitless attempt, though, as five minutes later he passed out.

Chapter 7

When Jack awoke, he was inside a building. The building, though, was crudely built and there were several weak spots. Next to him were his three katanas, the knife and dagger that he had in his boots and his backpack. He felt around his neck and saw that his pendant was still there. Outside he could hear howling winds worse than any storm he could recall. He sat up slowly and immediately felt pain. All over his body were tiny cuts where he didn't have clothes. His hands and face were covered in tiny slashes that seemed to be days old.

Ignoring the pain, Jack got up and looked around. A few feet farther away, Michelle was lying on a blanket, her staff beside her. Max and Selena were sleeping nearby leaned up against a wall. All of their belongings seemed to be with them. He didn't see Micheal though, but he did see Micheal's belongings. He tried sensing him through the mana but he only identified the four inside the building. Outside, the mana seemed to be behaving erratically and made it impossible to find any clear outlines.

Jack walked over to Michelle and saw for the first time that her face was deathly pale. This worried Jack. Although he never wanted a team, he was the captain and he was responsible for them. To add to this, they had spent three months fighting together and Jack realized then that he liked Michelle and would be sad if she died. He put his hand on her forehead and realized that she had a slight fever. He peered intently into the mana and realized then that her mana levels were extremely low.

"She'll be fine," said a gruff voice behind them. Micheal's voice.

"What happened, Micheal? Why is she like this? Why is her mana so low? Why am I covered in scratches?" Jack asked him.

Micheal looked into Jack's eyes for a second. He saw a flash of approval for a split second before he looked away abruptly. "Do you hear that wind outside?" Micheal asked.

"Yeah. Sounds like a storm," Jack replied.

"That's caused by the mana here. It's extremely potent but unstable. It's causing the elements to behave erratically. The wind here follows the flow of the mana and the flow of the mana makes it become tiny blades. You know those spells we perform that cut things with the wind?"

"Yeah..." Of course, Jack knew about that skill. It was one of his main skills.

"It's a natural phenomenon out there. But on a more tiny and precise scale. Millions of those things hit you at once, so without a mana skin, you get injured. It's worse because the mana is causing the wind to shift. If it was just mana, it could be cancelled, but since the wind has physical form, it's unavoidable. Understand?"

"Yeah," Jack said. "I let my mana skin drop and got cut."

"Yes. But it was more than just cut. Your clothes are enchanted to provide some semblance of protection. But every exposed place was badly slashed. And because it was the wind, we couldn't cancel the effects. We had to manually heal you. Rather, Michelle had to manually heal you."

"Oh," Jack said. Then it dawned on Jack. Millions of tiny cuts that weren't directly magic related. That means healing would have been extremely taxing. And if he wasn't healed, he would have died. "Oh my God. Michelle did that." Jack suddenly felt sick with himself. The extent that he had gotten injured caused Michelle to be in that state.

"Don't worry about it," Micheal said. "After you sent up the flares, we landed safely. If we had landed in the path we were originally on, we would have died. There wasn't anything there. We landed about three minutes after the second flare. We would have gotten here sooner but the first flare shot past us. We only caught a glimpse. When we saW the second, we immediately rushed to your location. There was more blood than we imagined. I started casting a protective barrier around you to stop the damage.

"While I was doing that, Michelle constructed this," and he gestured around the building, "It isn't pretty but it provides a bit of protection from the onslaught. We brought you inside and I stopped casting the protective barrier on you. I stepped out to put some protective spells on the shack to ensure it wouldn't suddenly collapse. Creation magic is extremely taxing, even to the strongest mages. When I came back in, Michelle had already started treating you. We couldn't stop it midway because it would be more dangerous. She held out just long enough to get you into the state you're in. Then she collapsed. She'll be out for a day or two while her mana recuperates."

Micheal finished his narration. Jack was at a loss for words. Two days. She'd be out for two days. Jack looked at Michelle for a few seconds, then looked at Micheal. He saw the same look of approval in Micheal's eyes before h abruptly headed for the door.

"I'm doing a bit of recon outside. Get something to eat and go to sleep. You aren't fully healed yet," then he walked outside, leaving Jack to his thoughts.

Chapter 8

After getting something to eat and getting some more sleep, Jack got up and decided to do some exploring. Selena and Max weren't in the shack and Michelle was the only one here. Micheal wasn't here either but maybe he hadn't returned from his reconnaissance yet. He knew his team could handle themselves out there. Jack sat on the floor of the shack and took off all of the clothes on his upper body except the chain with the pendant on it. He sat in a meditating position and started analysing the mana.

First, he looked at the mana within himself. He saw that he was back to normal. A little food and sleep always rejuvenated him.

Next, he examined Michelle. Her mana was extremely dense and brimming with energy. She was quickly recovering from her exertion.

Then he decided he was going to compare their mana. Jack's mana reserves were large but it wasn't as dense as Michelles. In fact, Jack's mana reservoir was a lot higher than Michelle's. He knew that his mana reserves were abnormal and that he had more mana than the average person, even among the highly trained. But the difference between his and Michelle's was like comparing the Dead Sea and the Atlantic Ocean. One was larger than the other, but the Dead Sea was potent enough to kill on touch. Jack concluded that they would be equal in ability as, even though he was bigger, the density of her mana made them equals.

After coming to this conclusion, he started checking the building and the contents. The building had a magical protection around it that kept from being torn apart by the wind. His clothes were intact and the magical protection placed on them held up. His backpack was also steadfastly strong along with Selena's, Max's, Micheal's and Michelle's.

There were no weapons in the room except for his three katanas and couple daggers. Michelle's staff was there as well. He inspected it closer, observing the flow of mana around it. As most sorcerers do, Michelle kept the large part of her staff erect while performing spells. The body of the staff was thin and long, almost five feet, and the head of the staff added another half foot. It was considerably thicker than the body and was shaped in a circle with spikes around it, much like the sun. The middle section protrudes outward giving the ball of the sun an almost spherical look. The spikes were all sharp enough to cut somebody and could be a dangerous weapon in combat. Mana swirled along the sun and condensed in the middle. There was a familiar feeling about the mana collecting there, but there were also some minute differences.

At the base of the staff intrigued him the most. He had once seen Michelle cast a spell with the butt of her staff. The base was separated from the body and formed a spike that was half a foot long, totalling the entire staff to be six feet long, a whole foot taller than its wielder. At the base of the staff, silver was the metal chosen for crafting and mana collected at the base. This mana, however, was darker than that of the head and was almost scary to behold. Jack figured that whatever was at the base opposed what was at the head and the placement was meant to not weaken the other.

After this, Jack studied the mana in the room and tried pulling it to himself. The mana quickly responded and flooded towards Jack. Before the mana could touch him though, he quickly stopped calling it. If he called all the mana in the room towards him it would create a vacuum that would quickly be filled by the mana outside and crush their protective shack.

Jack got up and walked outside, holding a firm mana skin around himself. Looking around he was surprised. He could barely see around him. He realized that without mana vision he was blind. He found a relatively open place with his feet and once again went into a meditating position. He made a sign with his hands ensuring that his mana skin would not be broken and he started meditating.

He felt around him and started controlling the mana. From erratic movements, the mana started slowing little by little until it came to a standstill, surrounding him with a thick layer. The mana in the Gateway was extremely dense, denser than Michelle's. Jack opened his eyes slowly, holding firm control of the mana. Around him, he could see in approximately a fifty-meter radius. He saw the shack they were staying in for the first time from the outside. He took careful account of his surroundings.

Around him were several large stones. Some were regular stones like he saw at the Gateway and some were made of a material he had never encountered before. Some were glowing with mana. It was similar to a mana infused blade, except these rocks had a lot more mana than any sword he had ever seen. The rock's themselves weren't built in any way special. The largest was Jack-sized, and Jack stood at a measly five foot eight. The smallest were no larger than his pendant.

The ground Jack was sitting on was sandy. He figured that the non-mana rocks he could see were being broken down to create the sand. He couldn't see the sky and he didn't see any water around him.

Jack called to the mana one more time, commanding it to stay still for ten minutes. He figured he had seven, with the chaotic environment. He walked around as fast as possible, gathering as much of the smaller rocks he could find. Upon inspection, Jack saw that there were several colours of the rock, including green, just like his pendant. He filled his pockets as fast as possible in five minutes and made his way back to the shack.

He unloaded his pockets and stood in the doorway, waiting for the mana to become wild again. He was counting the seconds in his mind. Seven minutes passed. Eight. Nine. Ten. Eleven. Then twelve. At twelve and a half the mana suddenly started to go back into a frenzy. It started slowly, frenzying inwards until the spot he had been sitting was filled.

The mana not only obeyed his command, it allowed him two and a half extra minutes.

Curious, Jack thought.

He then went inside and looked at the rocks he had gathered.

Chapter 9

Micheal, Max and Selena made their way into the shack quietly, so as to not awaken Jack and Michelle. However, when they walked through the door, they saw them both awake and looking at some rocks.

"You're awake," Micheal said, walking up to Michelle. Michelle got up and he hugged his sister tightly. "I was worried. That amount of mana was suicidal. Are you trying to die or something?"

"I'm fine, Mike," Michelle replied, her voice like a songbird. "It all worked out right?"

"Yeah yeah," Micheal said, his voice relaxing. "Just don't be so...so reckless, ok?"

"Yeah, ok Mike. Don't worry. I'm strong, remember," Michelle said.

"Yeah, I know," Micheal said, and let the matter drop. "Jack. We have some stuff to discuss."

"Yeah, we do," Jack replied. "Do you mind lighting a fire?"

Micheal looked at him curiously but held up his staff and started chanting, "Gather mana, and condense into this space. Change your nature and become warmth and strength, become fire." When he finished, he sat down next to it and rested next to him. "Ok sir. We have a lot to talk about."

"Yeah," Jack said. "First things first. Michelle, thanks. I'd have probably died if not for you."

"S-sure thing, Jack," Michelle said as she was sitting. Her face was red. "So, what else do we have to talk about?"

"Micheal, you start since you've been reconning the most," Jack said.

"No Max should begin," Micheal replied.

"Umm sure," Max said. Max was a big guy, basically the muscle of the team but he had a soft voice. "The rocks out there. I saw you brought some back. They give off an aura of mana that around it the mana becomes quiet. The bigger the rock the wider the area is cast."

"Yes," Selena said. She had a slightly nasal voice and a British accent. "The stones act like a homing point for the mana. We stopped near a big one and we were able to lower our mana skin without anything happening to us."

"So, we can use it for protection then," Michelle said.

"Exactly," Max said. "If we find some moderately sized rocks that we can carry we'll be able to go without anything happening to us."

"Hmm interesting," Jack said. "Just before Michelle woke up, I went outside and tried calming a portion of the mana. The mana obeyed me a little too well. I told it to stay still for ten minutes but instead it stopped for twelve and a half. I think the mana here is seeking stability but it can't find it."

"Makes sense," Michelle said. "Did you notice that the Gateway is expanding?"

"Umm no," Jack said. "What're you talking about exactly?"

"Well, it's like this Jack," Selena intervened. "We each went in with five to ten seconds between us. But the distance between where you landed and where we landed was almost fifty meters."

"And it's expanding on an upward movement," Max said. "The fall between what we felt and was increasing. We hit the ground at a higher level than you then walked downhill after you sent up that flare."

"I see. So, the movement between the Gateway left me in mid-air. But why?" Jack asked.

"Inertia," Max replied. "You entered at a specific point but you weren't in motion after passing through the portal, you just stopped in place."

"Ok yeah that makes a lot of sense," Jack said. "Wait so that means our destination is moving away from us. The longer we stay here the more we'll have to travel."

"Yeah, so we should get moving," Michelle said.

"One problem," her brother pointed out. "We still don't have enough protection."

"What? Jack collected plenty of stones though."

"The stones don't work like that. These stones are small. Stacking a bunch of same sized stones on top of each other will increase the strength of the barrier it makes but it won't increase the size. We need bigger stones than pebbles."

"So basically, it acts to make mana denser, not make your reserves bigger."

"Yup," Micheal said, confirming her point.

"Do the stones have elements?" Michelle asked.

"I'm sorry what?" Selena asked. "Elements? Like the periodic table?"

"No," Michelle said. "You don't know what elemental natures are?"

"Pretend I don't."

"Do you want to explain it or should I?" Michelle asked Micheal.

"You go ahead," Micheal replied.

"Ok sure. Do you two know what the elements are?" she directed at Jack and Max.

"I have a basic understanding but I'm sure you can add to my knowledge," Jack said invitingly.

"Same here," Max chimed in.

"Ok here's the basics. Mana can be converted into several forms. This is what we call magic. The eight basic elemental natures are wind, water, fire, earth, energy, yin and yang, light and darkness. All spells are derived from this. There are seven basic stones, called Affinity Stones, that are able to convert these and they're all colour coded; green, wind; water, blue; fire, red; earth, brown; energy, yellow; light, white; darkness black. Of course, white means actual white, not clear and black means black like obsidian not black diamonds. The stones make mana conversion easier and less taxing on the user so they can cast stronger spells easier."

"So, using obsidian will get you stronger spells?" Jack asked.

"No. It has to be magical obsidian. You can't just pick up any random rock and call it an Affinity stone," Micheal intervened.

"Exactly," Michelle affirmed, "Magic stones have certain mana properties about it that are very specific."

"So, the stones themselves have mana?" Jack asked.

"Yes and no. The stones have mana, yes, but when casting a spell, the stones gather natural mana and convert it to the element of the stone so the sorcerer doesn't exhaust his reserves. Only a stone with the element of the spell you're casting will activate."

"Understood," Jack said. "But there are other types of stones over there that aren't any of the colours you described."

"True," Michelle said. "Those stones are compound stones. They convert mana into a compound element like ice, smoke, lava, storm, etc. The downside of using this is that you can't separate the compound element so you can't use the root elements, so you can't cast earth or fire magic from a lava stone, only lava."

"Ok so is this a compound stone?" Max asked, pulling out his dagger. The blade was serpentine built and it was bright blue and shining. Jack looked at the hilt and saw that it was pure bronze, then at the pommel and saw that it was pure silver. The stone was the entire blue blade.

"Yes," Michelle said. "This is an ice stone. The largest ice stone I've ever seen."

"How about this?" Selena asked, pulling a grey stone pendant around from around her neck similar to Jack's green.

"Yes. That's a smoke stone," Micheal told her.

Jack then got up and went to his backpack and pulled out a knife. The knife had a small stone set to the base. "How about this?" Jack asked, showing her the white stone.

"That's a light stone," Michelle replied. "Our staff are also powered by the seven basic stones. Inside the head are the stones."

"Interesting," Jack said. "Are there any more stones?"

"Yes. There are legendary stones, like the spatial stones, as I'm sure you're aware of. Attempts have been made to replicate it but there is only one true spatial stone. The stone is capable of making breaks in space time to create portals. There's also the philosopher's stone. This stone doesn't change the mana but only gathers it. There's also the gravity stone which is able to manipulate gravity to the extent it can shift space time itself."

"What about Dark stones?" Selena asked.

"These stones are used by demons for dark magic. It corrupts the spells to turn it into dark spells. Dark isn't an actual nature. Anyone can use dark magic at any time with a stone but it can destroy the person if they aren't extremely strong. Demons and devils have a natural affinity for it so they can use it without inhibition."

"Why exactly is darkness not a spell?" Selena asked.

"Darkness is the absent of light. It's not something you can actively use," Micheal said to them.

"But what about Shadow Magic?" Max asked.

"Shadow magic is an example of Yin. It's a manifestation of the user's imagination in a non-physical object."

"Is cursed magic an example of Dark?" Selena asked.

"No, no it's not. Cursed magic can be any of the elemental releases. Including Dark. Cursed Magic is just corrupted Mana."

"What about Blood Manipulation?" Jack asked.

"Blood Manipulation is a manifestation of Yang, the ability to change the shape and structure of physical objects."

"I see."

The team sat back and digested this information for a second.

"Aren't there also stones that are used to heal or store magic?" Jack asked.

"Not exactly. Those are all imitations of the philosopher's stone. They aren't natural," Micheal told her. "Those stones all have a limit so it leaves scars after the process is finished. The philosopher's stone is able to completely undo any damage done."

"I see. So, it's basically a miracle in stone form?" Max responded.

"Yes. The Legendary stones are basically miracles."

"How many of them are there?"

"Eight."

"Ok, so, there are imitations of the philosopher's stone but what about the spatial stone and gravity stone?" Jack inquired.

"Well... as to that... there have been attempts at replicating the spatial stone but they failed. The gravity stone is a special case however..." Michelle trailed off.

"What she means is that there is only one known account of this gravity stone being in use but it isn't official and it's shrouded in mystery," Micheal picked up.

"One account?" Selena asked.

"Yes. I'm sure you know it. It's a human account. Everyone knows it," Micheal said, almost playful, testing them.

After a minute of them thinking, Max came to only one conclusion. "There is only one empire that fell to that degree that it was wiped out."

"What do you mean?" Jack asked. "There have been many empires that fell. Persia, Sparta, Rome, they all fell."

"Yes, but in this case the empire literally fell. Physically," Max replied.

"Ohhhh," Selena said, a look of dawning lighting up her face.

"I'm still confused," Jack said. He concentrated hard, but nothing came to mind.

"Atlantis," Max said.

"Correct," Micheal said.

"OHHH," Jack said. "That makes sense."

"Yup. It's our belief that the gravity stone was on Atlantis and when it activated it pulled the entire city down," Michelle said.

"We also believed that the gravity stone is at the bottom of the ocean with the city," Micheal finished her thought for her.

"Ok that's fine and all, but we really should get back on topic. We need to find a way to get out of here," Jack said, pulling them back to reality.

"Right, we really should," Max said.

"Ok so first things first are finding some stones that can cover us. And we need to do this fast because with the gateway expanding, we'll have to move quickly," Selena said.

"Not exactly," Jack replied. "I wasn't expecting you or Michelle to get this but I was expecting Max and Micheal to."

"Whatever do you mean?" Selena asked.

"Yeah, what are we supposed to get?" Max asked.

"Feel your face," Jack said. "You to Micheal."

Micheal's and Max's hand instantly shot to their face, feeling to see if something was wrong. After a few seconds, with them still rubbing their faces and a look of consternation on their faces, Michelle broke the silence, "What's wrong with them? I'm normal."

"No," Jack said. "They look exactly the same as when we entered."

"What?" Selena said, incredulously.

"Max, Micheal and I shave religiously, something I noticed over the last three months," Jack said.

"Ohh," Michelle said, then a slower, more thoughtful, "Ohhh."

"I still don't get it," Selena said.

"Well Selena, the facilities here aren't exactly the best for our hygiene. We can't exactly get a nice shave and haircut here," Jack said.

Selena still looked confused, prompting a response from Max, whose hand was still on his face, "None of us has even a tiny hair on our face right now."

"That's interesting and all but what exactly does that mean?" Selena said, growing angrier as this played out.

"It means," Micheal said, "We are exactly like how we entered, except for Jack who experienced negative effects in the space."

"So, we haven't aged, or changed at all since entering the Gateway," Max continued for Micheal.

"Which means that even though we experience time in here, we won't experience it in the same way that those on the other side of the Gateway does," Jack finished.

"So that means we can spend as long as necessary in here and it won't affect us or the outside," Michelle added, for Selena's benefit.

"So basically, we won't need to rush," Selena said, finally coming to the same conclusion as the others.

"Exactly," Jack said, "It also means we don't have to worry about food because as long as our body remains constant, we won't get hungry. Oh, and by the way, I don't think any of our watches are working. Mine isn't."

"Neither is mine," Selena said, "But I thought it was because of the mana in the air, honestly. It's good to know about the food thing though because we only had enough for five days."

They all agreed with this point as they all sat watching the fire in silence, no one wanting to be the one to break this moment of relief.

"So, what now?" Selena asked finally.

Everyone looked at Jack, waiting for his orders. After a minute of thought, Jack knew what they had to do.

"Michelle, Micheal and I will go out to find some good rocks," Jack said.

"About that," Micheal said. "Michelle and I can't go out together."

Jack looked at him and blinked twice, utterly confused. "What?"

"Out there, it's almost impossible to sense anything. The only way we made it back was because me and Michelle are connected so we can feel some of the things from each other and we can always sense each other," Micheal replied.

"Wait, you and Michelle can sense each other?" Jack said.

"Yeah. Almost all twins can do this. Just those with stronger mana can do it better," Michelle said, like it was common knowledge.

"Wait, all twins?" Jack asked.

"Yeah, all twins," Micheal said.

Jack sat there and digested that for a second, thinking about what exactly that meant.

"Ok ok. Michelle, Max and I will go," Jack said, after a moment. "Selena, I hope you don't mind since you already had a chance to explore a bit. You as well Micheal."

"No problem, Jack," Micheal said. "I have to warn you though. You have no sense of direction out there. Stick together and if you do split up, you'll need to send out mana that's stronger than the surroundings to get pinpointed. I'll find Michelle easily and Max has an abnormal amount of mana but you need to be careful ok. The door opens in the direction of the gateway we came through. Decide where you go after that."

"Ok," Jack said. "I'll be careful. Let's go guys."

***

"Max, I have a question," Jack said.

They were about a kilometre from the shack, and every two hundred meters or so, Jack would stop and calm the mana enough to identify any potential rocks in the area. So far, they had collected two and needed three more. They walked in silence so as to not unconsciously break their mana skins.

"Yeah, what's up Jack?" Max replied.

"Well," Jack began. "You're totally fit and stuff but I never see you use a sword and you aren't carrying one now. Over the last three months I've only seen you use that dagger."

"Oh," Max said, as if he was expecting a harder question. "Well, the dagger is made of ice stone and it compliments my abilities. I've trained with it for all my life so I'd say I'm just as capable of fighting with it as you are with a sword."

Jack laughed. "Don't kid yourself Max. We've fought five times and you lost all of them."

"Ok true," Max said, with a half-smile on his face. "Maybe I'm more on Selena's level."

This made Jack laugh again. "No Max. Not even close."

Max started laughing. "What, you don't think I can beat Selena?" Max asked jokingly.

"Of course not," Jack said. "Hell, I can't beat Selena myself, in a standard sword fight at least."

They both laughed at this. Even though Selena was smaller than the two men, she was by far more skilled with a sword.

"You know, I did train with a sword. Well, sort of," Max said after they both stopped laughing.

"Really?" Michelle asked.

"Yeah," Max said. "Back when I was younger, I met this Russian guy with a sword when my dad took me there. Long story short, I liked it and I got a machete. It's twenty-six inches in length and I keep it in my bag."

"So why don't you carry it everywhere with you?" Jack asked. "And how come you've never fought me with it before?"

"Well, as for the first, I have the dagger," Max said slowly. "As for the second, it's because one hit and your swords will shatter."

This got Jack laughing. "My blades will shatter? As if."

"No, I'm serious. Russian bladesmiths put soft steel together with hard steel back-to-back in their swords. The construction causes the hard steel to pull back on the soft steel in the hardening process. Well anyway, after twenty years of using it and running my mana through it, it started retaining my magical properties. The difference in mana causes anything it touches to break apart."

"Oh wow," Jack said. "Well...that's pretty interesting. Let's stop for a minute and look for some stones."

After calming the mana, Jack and the others found one more suitable stone. They put it in the bag Max was carrying and got ready to move again. Jack waited until the mana started back its usual frenzy, timing it to see how long it'd take. Always the result was two to three minutes longer than the time Jack told it to.

After of setting off, Jack started speaking again. "How about you Michelle? Do you carry any weapons or just the staff?" Jack already knew the answer but he wanted to see what she'd say.

Just then, they started going uphill. As they had agreed before, after reaching the rise, they went parallel to it.

"Umm yeah, I carry a knife inside my robes," Michelle said. She took it out to reveal an eight-inch blade with a serrated back edge, generally the type hunters use. The blade itself was made of bronze.

"Can I see that?" Max asked.

"Sure," Michelle said, handing the blade over. Max examined it for a second and handed it over to Jack.

"What's wrong?" Jack asked, taking the blade. When he took it, he stopped walking, causing the other two to stop as well. The blade felt heavy in his hands, and the aura surrounding it was dark.

"This blade- it's cursed," Jack said. "It's more cursed than my own cursed sword."

"Yeah," Max said. "More cursed than my dagger as well. Michelle, can you use that?"

"Yeah," Michelle said, "It's no different than a kitchen knife to me."

The two boys looked at her as if she just sucker punched them. "What? What's the big deal with cursed blades? It looks normal to me," she said, wilting under their looks.

"Michelle, do you understand how cursed blades work?" Max asked her uncertainty.

"No, not really," Michelle replied.

Jack looked at Max and asked him, "Do you want to explain to her?"

"Umm sure," Max said. The look on his face wasn't pleasant. When speaking of cursed blades, swordsmen almost always felt guilty. "Basically, during the forging process, while heating the metal, the bladesmith introduces a bit of blood into the blade. The blade retains a bit of the personality of the owner of the blood. Cursed blades have a life of their own and they take some coaxing when they are called into action. If the blade doesn't like the user, it can turn on them and cause them to die. My own ice dagger is cursed."

"So is my Hogo," Jack said.

"Ok and? If you both use cursed blades, why are you so against me using one?" Michelle replied hotly.

"Michelle, to control a cursed blade, the user has to coax it to work. Usually that means force it or earn its trust. The stronger the curse, the more the user has to exert control over it. I forced my blade into submission but well...," Jack said slowly, trying to calm her.

"Ok so?" Michelle said, growing angrier at the way Jack was talking to her.

"Michelle, the curse on this blade is twenty times stronger than my dagger," Max said quickly, as if the truth was forcibly ripped from his throat.

"And it's almost one hundred and fifty times stronger than Hogo," Jack said.

"W-what?" Michelle said, her anger abated. "It's that bad?"

"Yeah. It's almost as if while making this blade they killed someone over the forge and drained their blood into the bronze," Max said. "A really big person. Bigger than me."

"And more dangerous than all of us combined," Jack added.

Michelle froze, her mind working, trying to think up an explanation why there would be so much blood in the knife that wasn't so grotesque. "Maybe they introduced the blood at different times, a little at a time over a really long period, or the donor extracted blood several times and introduced it when he collected a lot."

"No," Jack said, his face grim. "The aura around the blade is heavy. The blood was forced out of the person all at once, against his will."

"I'm sure that I'd never be able to use this knife," Max said.

"And with even my expertise I wouldn't risk it in a thousand years," Jack said. "It's a wonder how you can use it Michelle, much less be oblivious. That knife would try as hard as possible to kill the user with all the pent-up anger in that blade."

He handed the blade back to Michelle and looked at her. She was struck dumb as she had no idea what to say.

Chapter 10

Jack was putting on his shirt. With no other way to break the silence after that heavy information drop, Jack decided to search the area for stones, to no avail. Including a part of someone's life was common in the creation of swords, but speaking about it was always an uncomfortable experience for anyone. Part of this was that no one knew what happened to the person whose life was used to make the sword. Sealing part of a person's blood meant sealing part of their lifeforce and no one knew what happened to these persons. It was often believed that this practice sealed their faith to a life of battle.

The three explorers went on, heading in a general direction hoping to stumble across some rocks. The silence was like a bomb as they weren't quite ready to start another conversation. Jack noticed that Max was thinking hard about something though, so he waited for him to speak. After a few moments, he did.

"Jack, you noticed that we weren't changing. Any idea why?" he asked.

"Yes, I think I have one," Jack replied.

"How about you Michelle?" Max asked her.

"I think it's just the magic of the place," Michelle said, then paused. "But you two think something else, right," looking at them expectantly, waiting for a reply.

Max and Jack said nothing, waiting for the other to reply first. Finally, Max responded.

"Yes. How much do you know about quantum physics?" Max began.

Jack looked at him, with an expression between amusement and mild surprise. "I know quite a bit about quantum physics. But actually, I was thinking about something else...magically created wormholes."

Max's eyes widened, "That's good. Do you have a hypothesis?"

"Yeah, I do," Jack replied, the intrigue making his eyes twinkle. "Shall we compare?"

"We shall," Max replied, his voice raising a few octaves as he started getting excited. "Michelle, do you have any ideas or...."

"Oh no," Michelle replied. "You two go ahead. This is way out of my ball park."

"Ok then," Jack said. "Open the floor Mr. Kori," referring to Max by his last name.

"Very well then, Mr. Drake," Max replied with the same structure. "Basically, I think the gateway is one entrance to a quantum tunnel, which we are inside now. Quantum travel involves particles entering and existing the same way, as carbon copies of each other with no discernible change."

"Interesting," Jack replied. "But you see, if this were a quantum tunnel, it wouldn't have injured me like it did. Quantum tunnels should leave the 'travellers' in one constant state until they exit."

"Good point," Max said. "But you see, we're larger than a particle. And it's true that particles remain the same, but complex structures don't necessarily follow this principle. The particles of your body may remain the same inside the space, but the structure may change."

"True," Jack said. "But here's why I think it's a wormhole. Because of the theory of relativity, our watches have stopped. Inside a wormhole, matter doesn't necessarily remain constant because it's unnatural. Also, wormholes are created from an intense event that renders a tear in space time, causing the crazy mana that we're seeing."

"Interesting, but here's the thing," Max said, rising to the challenge. "The passageway is expanding. If it was a worm hole it would be a constant rip in space time and a passageway of the same size continuously."

Jack's eyes were twinkling. "That's a good point. However, you should realize that if it was quantum tunnelling, it would be near instantaneous, unlike a wormhole, which would require a bit of time inside of the passageway because it is a rift in space time not just space. Wormholes abide by the laws of time, unlike quantum teleportation."

As they went on, their manner of speaking slowly became that of academic speech, almost as if they were two professors explaining a topic in a lecture hall. They were slowly getting more and more invested in the topic, all thought of magic stones and cursed bladed forgotten.

"Au contraire, Mr. Drake," Max replied, the excitement in his voice making him speak faster, "You see, based on my hypothesis of quantum tunnelling, it should be that movement is instantaneous, but only if energy is constant. We came in faster than we are moving now and we're going in the opposite direction than we came in, so technically we're facing barriers in our travel."

"I like that," Jack said, a mischievous smirk on his face. "In fact, that makes so much sense that I don't have a rebuttal. But I will point out that there are rocks like the entrance in here, meaning that the passageway is emitting a gravitational field."

"That's pretty good, I'll give you that," Max said, losing his edge. "I didn't consider the non-magical rocks." Max walked in silence, stroking his chin, thinking of a comeback. "Ok," he said at last, his voice dejected. "You got me."

Jack laughed. "Don't be disheartened. This is science not magic. We need to keep collecting data. But I like your hypothesis. It's pretty smart."

"Wait a second!" Max exclaimed suddenly. An idea came to him in an instant. "We aren't aging. If it were a wormhole, we'd still be aging, but time has stopped!"

Jack laughed again. He was enjoying this, "Good one. Too bad for you that I thought of that. Time is just moving extremely slow for us but it is moving. The delicate nature of the wormhole is interfering with our watches which are electronic. Time dilation will make us age, but it will be at a slower rate than on the other side of the gates and it's almost unnoticeable, even to us."

"Oh yeah," Max said dejectedly, realizing that Jack's theory was air tight. He walked with his head down in defeat for a while then suddenly he stopped and his head shot up. Michelle bumped into Max and they all stopped. "Jack," he said, his voice low and deadly serious, "You better hope your theory is wrong. If we are inside a wormhole, then time is passing all around us. The breakdown and war are still happening."
Jack absorbed his words, realizing the truth in it. He suddenly hoped everything he thought was wrong. "Let's get those stones and get out of here as fast as possible," Jack said, with utter determination in his voice.

Chapter 11

The trio finally gathered enough stones for everyone and headed back to the shack. When they arrived, Jack ordered everyone to get prepared to leave.

"What's with all this information dump all at once. I feel like a novice adventurer again!" Selena exclaimed after Jack and Max narrated their recent guesses to the group.

They decided that, even though they had the stones, they would keep their mana skins active at all times, in case they lost their stones or it failed on them. Securing the stones on their backpacks with some string, they headed out into the whirlwind.

They trudged along in silence, determined to get to the other side of the gateway as possible. Every so often, Jack would break the pace to allow them a break by calming the mana and allowing them to loosen their mana skin for a bit of time. In these times, Max would activate mana eyes and survey as far as possible, hoping to find some form of life, always to no avail.

Eventually, after what felt like days, Jack and company finally made it to the other side of the gateway with no major incidents that they could note.

Stepping through the exit gateway, Jack was greeted with an attack. The guards at this gateway, seemingly unaware that they were coming through, suddenly drew their swords and rushed Jack. Jack immediately sprang into action, drawing his tool steel swords and intercepting the attack.

One guard, heavy set and bearing an axe rushed Jack head on. Jack caught the attack with both swords and crossed it, locking the axe into place. This left his back exposed to any attack from behind. He wasn't worried though, as between him and the gate was about two meters total and only a very tiny man would be able to fit in that space, much less swing a sword.

Unfortunately, he was wrong and his senses picked up someone behind him, who wasn't in his party. From the outline of the mana that Jack could sense, the man was tiny, standing only around four feet. With no other option, Jack gathered the mana into his back and arms and braced himself for full impact. The sword blow that landed glanced off of him, light enough that the congealed mana threw the sword at him, effectively deflecting the attack but still tearing his shirt and jacket.

This surprised Jack a little, as he was expecting a heavier sword blow. However, he didn't waste this opportunity. He took a quick step back, pulling his right foot back and going down onto his knees, upsetting the axe-man. He followed Jack, his feet now unsteady and his centre of balance focused onto the axe, which he was focusing all of his power on. Jack then twisted his upper body directing the axe to his left and focused the power into his right foot, suddenly rising and completely making the axe-man fall off of him, plummeting to the ground with no hope of rising. Jack raised his sword in his right hand and, turning it so that the blunt edge faced down, he landed a blow onto the axe-man's neck, knocking the man unconscious.

Not wasting a minute, Jack turned on his heel to the tiny swordsman who was preparing to stab him from behind. He caught the blow from the sword, running the blades along each other until it caught in the guard of his sword. He followed this action by raising his opponent's sword, breaking his stance and aiming a roundhouse kick into his opponent's head with enough force to make his helmet chime like a bell. He brought his foot down into a full arc and smashed his head into the ground, ending the fight.

The swordsman whose swords he had deflected earlier came rushing at him. He counted four of them in total. They were all wearing full body armour and covered their body entirely. They were all between four and five feet, the tallest maybe four foot nine. Not wanting to waste time, he crossed his swords in front of his body, running his mana through the blades. When he was satisfied with the concentration, he slashed his blades in an "X" motion as fast as possible. The resulting shockwave from this rapid motion cut the air in front of him, knocking the approaching knights in its stream.

Suddenly an arrow came hurtling towards him, catching his cheek in its arc. A wound opened up that seared with pain and a small fire suddenly caught at his feet. Jumping aside to make sure his pants leg did not catch on fire. He looked up and saw that above him six archers were aiming arrows down on him and chanting spells. He raised his sword to deflect the arrow as one let an arrow go aimed at his chest. Raising his sword, he caught the arrow in mid-air, thinking he could deflect it. Instead, the arrow exploded into a white cloud, blocking his vision as dust clouded his eyes. Blinded, he heard another arrow whiz past his left ear and felt the ground go wet near his leg.

"Mana come to me and take the form of wind, take shape and form a barrier, protect my comrade," Jack heard behind him. It was Michelle, who had emerged from the portal in the midst of the fight.

He sensed the others following her close behind. "Don't kill them," he shouted in desperation.

"Mana collect and take the form of ice, now form bullets with blunt edges and rush my enemies, seis prisas," Max yelled from behind Jack. The air grew cold and he could feel the water at his feet growing colder. He felt a rush of air as the bullets soared past quickly striking the airborne archers.

"Mana come to me and take the form of fire, create a barrier to protect my comrades and myself from our enemies," Micheal yelled and Jack felt a wave of heat on his face as fire sprung up in front of them.

"Go to sleep," Selena yelled. A wave of fatigue rushed over everyone within earshot. Jack issued a thin stream of water from his finger tips, washing his eyes and waking himself up.

Regaining his vision, Jack saw several bodies around them as the fire dissipated which were protecting them. Several knights were coming up with swords and awes drawn, although they were a bit disheartened by the view they received.

"Selena translate our languages," Jack yelled over the noise.

"We understand each other," Selena yelled back. A wave ice cold wind rushed over the area.

"Wait!" Jack yelled. "Cease your attacks. We come in peace." He hoped Selena's spell worked.

One knight, dressed in red, came up to the front of the knights with his sword drawn in front of him. "You attacked my men," he said, his voice heavy.

"We were defending ourselves," Jack called out. This man was obviously the leader of the knights here. "All your men are alive and unharmed, except for a few bruises. Please listen to us."

The knight looked at Jack, assessing the situation. "Very well," he said finally. "State your name and purpose."

Jack took a breath, preparing himself. "I am Jack Dawson, of the house Dawson of the human realm. We've come to claim a human treasure that is kept in this realm to stop the invasion of the demon race."

"I need identification," the knight said, his voice cold.

"Ok," Jack said. He sheathed the sword in his left hand then reached into his left pocket and pulled out a ring on a chain with a crest on it. The crest featured a Jackdaw and twin pieces of olives on either side. The knight walked up and looked at the crest on the ring.

"Very well," he conceded. "Identify your comrades."

"This is Max Kori, of house Kori, Micheal and Michelle Bacht, twin mages and..." he trailed off. He didn't know Selena's last name even though they'd known each other since they were starting adventurers.

"Selena Conan, of the Conan family," Selena picked up in his break in speech.

Jack's eyes widened slightly, realizing who she was. "Do you need identification for them as well?" Jack finished.

"No, that will not be necessary, Mr Dawson," the knight said. "Come with me. I'll take you to meet the Chancellor in charge of this area." He then turned to his men, "Weapons down boys. Tend to the wounded." He then led a path through the soldiers, and Jack followed him, not looking back at his team, not wanting to see the looks in their eyes.

Chapter 12

The chancellor was a large man seated behind a desk. His skin was blue and he had wings on his back. He stood at foot tall and his hair was short, cropped to his skull and a bright shade of green. The knight who led them here also had wings on his back but he could make out nothing else about the man as he was dressed fully in black clothing. They had truly entered fairy territory.

"I am Darius Billent, Chancellor of this area. I understand that you are Jack Dawson and company?"

"Yes sir, we are."

"Quite frankly Mr. Dawson, we believed you dead."

"Dead? Why?" Max asked.

"It has been a week since you were first expected to arrive here, Mr. Kori."

"That's-" Jack was at a loss for words. So was everyone else in his company.

"What's happened in the last week?" Michelle asked.

"And why were we attacked?" Micheal added.

"You have had no news?"

"No. Nothing," Selena said.

"The Demons have taken more of Eden. Few demons were spotted on Earth, presumed to be scouts. Earth sent a group of knights to find out what was going on, but only three returned of the six. Those three...were not in the best shape."

"What do you mean?" Jack asked.

"You know of the zombie people?" Darius asked.

"Sort of. They're the ones who returned from Eden in a dreamlike state believing that the Demons should take Eden right?" Jack questioned.

"Yes. It was quite the strange phenomenon. Eden was invaded but not a single person was injured, at least not demon inflicted wounds."

"Right, the majority of the injured were caused by the magic beasts that came through with the Demons," Selena pointed out.

"Correct, but even those were given medical attention," Michelle pointed out.

"Yes, it was the least violent takeover ever seen in the last thousand years," Darius said. "This has confused us for quite some time."

"So, what's going on now? What's happening?" Jack asked impatiently.

"These zombie people have sort of awoken from a trance. They're insisting that Eden be given to the Demons," Darius explained.

"Right, we already knew that. But what about the scouts?" Jack asked.

"The knights who went exploring, well the ones who returned, they weren't quite the same. One of them was badly injured and was carried by his peers to safety. He hasn't regained consciousness."

"And the others?"

"They aren't the same anymore. They started speaking about some Darkness and it was very...I'm not sure how to describe it. They saw something but they can't say what. Not because something is binding their tongues, but like they can't process what it was they experienced."

"The Darkness? Do they mean Dark?" Micheal asked.

"Like the magic Dark?" Selena asked.

"Yes," Micheal said.

"We don't know," Darius said. "We assumed so, but they're not doing so good."

"What else happened?"

"Nothing out of the ordinary. Magic beasts broke through different Pathways that sprang up but they've so far been contained."

"Ok. Mr Billent, we'd like to get ready to go collect the artifact that we came for. We were told that the Fairy Queen would help us."

"I see, Mr Dawson-"

"Jack."

"-Jack. You see, first we'd like to know what happened inside of the Pathway you used. It was previously deemed as too dangerous to use but we'd like to use it to send troops to Earth to reinforce the Guard there."

"The Pathway, huh. Where do I even begin." They sat in Billent's office a while longer discussing what happened inside the Pathway. They also discussed means of travel and lodging for the night, as the sun was starting to set.

Billent called a soldier into his office. "Set Jack here," he said, indicating Jack, "And his team up for the night. Send a knight at once to the castle informing them that some extremely important guests have arrived and that they need a meeting as fast as possible. Next, make arrangements for a place for them to stay in the capital and travel arrangements for them to leave at first light tomorrow. I hope these accommodations are to your liking?" Billent finished, looking at Jack.

"I was hoping we could leave today," Jack replied.

"Impossible," Billent said. "The sun is about to set and the forest can be very dangerous at night. Spend the night in our town."

"Very well," Jack said. "I guess one night wouldn't hurt, but I must insist that our mode of transport be as fast as possible."

"That can be arranged," Billent replied.

"One last thing. I'd like some provisions. Some clothes that are durable and protective, similar to our leather but not inhibiting any magic. I'm sure there are materials like that here that have been fabled even in our lands."

"Indeed," Billent said, smiling. "Good to know that our products are famous in your world."

"Yes," Jack went on. "I would also like three daggers, you decide the materials but ensure that they are able to withstand high amounts of mana, as well as one short sword, single edged and two short swords, double beveled. And for our sleeping arrangements, I'd like everyone to have easy access to each other, but separate the boys from the girls."

"Very well. All of this can be done to your liking," Billent said, fully compliable with a smile on his face.

***

After a full three course meal and a night of deep sleep, Jack and his team woke up ready to take on the day. The new clothes were left outside of their room in bags made of straw and the new weapons were outside in a box made of wood. Jack took the box of weapons into his room and took the clothes tagged with his name on it.

He washed his face in the basin full of water and spread the clothes out on his bed. There were black pants made of a strong material that couldn't be pulled apart easily, but it was soft and warm. The material was made from a particular tree's fruit which collected sunlight. The tree was called Daemchheu Rreahatit, the sun tree. The fruit had fibres inside of it similar to cotton but it was stronger and it was always warm as it constantly held solar radiation. There was a long-sleeved jersey of the same material, dyed red.

Next, he pulled out a long black coat with a scaly pattern that he identified as dragon skin. The fairy realms were home to the most dragons in the nine realms since fairies didn't actively hunt them for sport like humans did. Dwarves often caught dragons for the sake of manufacturing products, but fairieds only used dead dragons to harvest skin from. Dragon skin had unique properties as well. They were extremely strong and durable, able to shatter weaker blades on impact, and it boosted magical properties.

Jack unsheathed each sword one by one, inspecting them. The metals were a bronze colour, but unlike the yellow metals of earth, these were extremely strong. When Jack ran a knife along the edge, not a scratch appeared on the surface. He vaguely recalled that the metal was called Saamritth Meas.

Afterwards, he pulled out the three daggers. Their blade lengths were eight inches, and they had vine patterns running along the handle. The metal of the blades glowed a bright blue, similar to ionized titanium. He identified the weapon as Rungrous Khiev. This blade was able to boost magical properties.

He kept a dagger for himself, then placed a dagger each in Selena and Max's bag of clothes, along with the single edged shortsword for Max. The two double edged shortswords would take on Micheal and Michelle as companions.

Chapter 13

After eating breakfast and inspecting their new weapons, the team headed out on Pegasi for the capital, Thirén. Billent had been able to secure five Pegasi for their use since it would be faster and they could make up for the time they'd lost in the Gateway.

The Pegasi flew at a blinding rate, comparable to maybe a Cessna. Soon Thirén came into view. The great tree-borne city was housed in the largest tree in the nine worlds, the Daemccheu Pised, Yggrassil. The tree stood at almost eleven thousand five hundred feet and had golden leaves and an orb like fruit that grew on it. The branches spread almost one thousand feet in diameter. At the head of the tree, the fairy queen lived in a castle made of a strange silver rock that could only be found in the fairy realm.

Seven smaller trees, called Tech Pised, housed the rest of the capital. At the head of each Tech Pised, a noble family lived. In the lower branches of both the Daemccheu Pised and the Teches Pisedies housed several fairies and trading posts where goods were sold. Hanging off the branches were cages in which criminals were kept for public humiliation, a practice that was still carried on in the fairy realm.

As Jack and his team entered the upper regions of Yggdrasil, he looked down to see workers of the noble houses look up at him. Fairies with green, grey and red skin looked up at him, their hair dazzling in shades of blue, silver, green and orange. Some were hovering as their translucent wings hummed on their backs, and some were on the ground tending to the grounds. Jack passed over the black castle heading ever upwards towards the Daemccheu Pised, where he had a meeting with the queen.

***

The Pegasi flew gracefully through the sky and landed with equal grace. The Pegasus that Jack was riding on was coal black and his tail flew gracefully in the wind behind him. His wings beat with the grace of an angel. Literally the only word that came to Jack's mind was graceful. But to him he didn't need another word. Their entire existence was graceful. The Pegasus set Jack down on a field with several other Pegasi. He was the first to land and dismount.

He looked around. There were several guards and some Pegasi were in the same field he set down on. Further on were walls surrounding the castle. The walls were shining white. The air was dense with extremely potent mana and the air was exceptionally fresh, unlike anything that he could find on earth.

Jack heard something behind him. He turned around and saw a guard rushing him with a sword. Halfway drawing his sword, he caught the blade of the knight's sword inches from his neck with the tip of his sword still in the scabbard. Jack took a step back, trying to put some distance between them, but bumped into the Pegasus he just dismounted. The guard took a step towards him, closing the slight gap he created and put his whole weight on his sword. Both of Jack's hands were preoccupied making sure he didn't get decapitated and the guard was a whole head shorter than Jack so a headbutt was out. He was in a tough spot. He had two options; push back and try to trip the guard risking a slit throat, or wait for his team.

His team was still in the air, so he was going to trip the guard. Fully drawing his sword without any shift in the lock that existed between them, Jack hooked his foot on the guard's and pushed back. The guard fell hard on his knees. Jack took the butt of his sword and struck the guard on the head, directly on his blue forehead, and knocked him unconscious.

Jack took a few steps forward to put some space between him and the Pegasus so he could swing his sword. Surprisingly, he didn't see any other guards advancing towards him. He looked up because the others hadn't landed yet and saw them being intercepted by fairies.

Michelle fired off several projectiles at the fairies in the air but they dodged. Micheal and Selena tried to break away from the group and tried to circle around behind them but they were intercepted and shot at. Max pulled out his dagger and conjured a shield of ice in front of them before they got hit. Taking advantage of Max's distraction, one of the fairies fired a fireball at him, which Michelle deflected with a blast of air.

The Fairies zipped through the air quickly and they were more agile than the Pegasi so they were getting the upper hand. Jack looked around once more and saw that no one made a move towards him, he drew his other two swords and prepared to help his team. He placed Hogo in his mouth, gripping it with his teeth. Then he raised the tool steel swords and threw them as hard as possible in the air towards the fairies. By controlling the wind around them, Jack made them spin in the air towards the fairies attacking his teammates.

One of his swords was coming in for an attack but the fairy dodged neatly out of the way. The creatures were nimble, he had to admit. Their wings beat quickly like hummingbirds and they were translucent so he couldn't judge the direction they were going to turn in the air. This posed a problem to Jack because if he couldn't predict the patterns of the enemy, he couldn't counter attack.

Jack removed the sword from his mouth and held it tightly in his left hand. He then directed his airborne swords to make circles around his teammates to create a barrier from any solid attacks that headed straight towards them.

Seeing this, the fairies let out a furious assault of fire and rocks headed their way, but strangely not taking notice of Jack. The fairies on the ground also seemed to not care what Jack was doing. This suited Jack perfectly. Focusing the mana in his feet, he released it with an explosive burst and leaped high into the air. When his ascent stopped, he focused the mana on his right leg, then converted it to wind nature and kicked off, propelling himself upwards. He repeated this with his left leg and kept repeating the process effectively allowing him to walk on air.

He directed both his swords towards an attacking fairy holding a staff causing the fairy to change directions and disrupting his next attack. Jack got behind him and slashed at him, using the back of his sword to hit him squarely on the neck. The fairy careened out of the air, the sheer force of the blow sending him crashing into the ground. The fairy behind him sent a hail of rocks at him but Jack directed his two airborne swords to intercept the attack, effectively blocking it.

Using the opening Jack created, Selena unsheathed her sword and pointed it at the fairy. The blade glowed a brilliant silver in the sunlight and in a second a thin stream of light issued from her sword, soaring at the fairy and leaving a hole in his leg two inches in diameter. The fairy, overcome with pain, fainted and started falling. This caused another fairy to leave the formation and dive to catch her before she crashed.

The remaining three fairies numbered three and they stopped buzzing about the air. Micheal raised his staff and chanted a quick spell under his breath and in the next instant a black liquid that looked extremely sticky and viscous issued from his staff and covered the fairy he was aiming at. The fairy, now covered in the liquid, fell out of the air since he couldn't move his wings.

Max swiped his dagger in the air and the air in his path froze, the water droplets in the air solidifying. The first fairy he hit was covered in little pieces of ice and the weight of the ice on his wings caused him to stop flapping and caused him to fall as well. The second fairy ascended in a second, his foot being the only thing caught in the attack.

Jack made his way over to the fairy, swiping at him but moved nimbly to the right. Jack jumped upwards over the fairy and began a freefall headfirst. The cold of Max's spell chilled his lungs and as he lined up with the fairy, he looked him in the eye with a cold look, a thin stream of mist issuing from his mouth as he slashed his sword, the back of the blade catching the fairy's neck and throwing him to the ground.

Jack flipped in the air and issued a stream of wind from his feet to hover in the air. "Land quickly. We can fight better on the ground," he shouted.

His team did as was ordered while Jack observed from above. Soldiers started approaching them from all sides surrounding his team as they dismounted, preparing for battle. Jack surveyed the area and saw a single hooded figure observing the fight with two guards at his side.

Jack sped towards him. He aimed his sword at his throat and stopped with the sword touching his throat, the resulting force sending a wave of air to unhood the figure.

The fairy gave Jack a mysterious smile. "Call them off," he said through gritted teeth, his voice cold.

The fairy queen raised her hand and at a signal from the guard at her side, all the soldiers stopped short.

Chapter 14

"You're holding your sword to a queen's throat you know," the Fairy Queen said.

"And if that queen is smart, she'll tell her soldiers to stand down," Jack said slowly, anger coming through with each word.

The queen made a signal with her hands and the guards that were near them lowered their hands from their swords.

"We've been here two days and we've been attacked twice," Jack said angrily.

"It was a test," the Queen said.

"Why?" Jack asked through gritted teeth, his sword not budging an inch.

"Why do you think?" the Queen replied, challenge in her eyes. "What if you were incompetent? Are we going to leave the faith of the world, all the worlds, in your hands?"

"We are all S-Ranked Adventurers. You think we aren't capable of killing everyone here?" Jack said coldly. He removed his sword from the queen's throat and turned his back on her, heading towards his team.

***

Jack and his team entered the castle halls. All around them were knights and servants roaming the silk lined walls.

As Jack and the others walked up to the doors leading to the throne room, a guard stopped them by crossing their spears in front of the doors. "You aren't allowed to carry weapons into the throne room," the guard on the right said.

"Go tell your queen that there have already been two attempts on our lives and we'll be keeping our weapons," Jack replied, his voice cold enough to freeze an ocean.

The guards looked at one another and the one on the right called another guard in the hall and whispered something to him. The guard rushed off down the hall to, conceivably, carry the message. After ten minutes or so, the guards at the door uncrossed their weapons and allowed them to enter.

Jack led his party into the main throne room. It was a long room with a red carpet down the centre leading up to a main throne made of gold and leather. To the sides were six smaller seats, three to each side, that were made of silver and less impressive than the throne.

On the throne sat the fairy queen, her green skin and red hair glowing in the sunlight streaming in from the windows on the roof. She was wearing purple robes and held a sceptre made of gold inlaid with a diamond. The six smaller seats were all empty.

"No need to bow," the fairy queen said, her voice high. "There's no one here besides us. Something you should be happy for since with my presence alone would be unable to keep your weapons."

"We weren't going to leave our weapons. You attacked three nobles unprovoked," Jack replied. "With the current war taking place, your realm won't be able to sustain a second war with our people," Jack replied.

The queen pursed her lips. "Yes well, it's rather unfortunate that you think that way but a test had to be conducted."

"Well since you felt the need to conduct a test, you must already know what we're here for."

"I do."

"That makes things easier then." Jack reached into his bag and pulled out a scroll, which he held out in his hand.

Holding out her hand and waving her fingers, the scroll located through the air and into her hands. She unrolled the scroll and began reading. When she finished, she looked up at Jack. "You do know that this is no easy task?"

"I do. But it is necessary," Jack replied.

"Very well, Mr Dawson. You and your team may retrieve the Spatial Stone. Have dinner with me tonight. I will make arrangements for you to stay in the castle and for your travels myself. You shall leave within the week," the Queen decreed.

"Why must we wait a week longer? Isn't the situation urgent enough to require immediate action?"

"It will take you at least a week to acclimate to the mana of this world, given that you are competent enough. You go tomorrow and you will never come back. Many skilled adventurers would take longer."

Jack considered the situation. Truthfully, he could sense a difference in the mana here as opposed to Earth. Earth's mana was thick and cloudy, like smoke, but here it was dense and light, like fog. "Very well. A week should be sufficient," Jack said. "But I need to hear you say it. Say you give us permission and that you treat us as guests to your kingdom."

The queen looked angry at this statement. "You do not trust me, Mr Dawson?"

"My team and I were attacked twice already. If it were myself alone, I would be fine. I can fight your entire army alone. But say it for my team to hear. Make the unbreakable declaration."

"We are alone. There are no witnesses," the Queen said.

"The mana will be our witness," Jack replied.

"Very well," the queen conceded. "I, Amaryllis Sindervelt, hereby decree that Jack Dawson, Selena Conan, Max Kori, Michelle Bacht and Micheal Bacht are guests to our nation and no one shall harm them. I hereby give full consent for Jack Dawson, Selena Conan, Max Kori, Michelle Bacht and Micheal Bacht to seek the Spatial Stone which resides in this realm. No citizen of this country will bring harm to these five with malicious intent, or he will be outcasted."

"Thank you, Your Majesty," Jack said, bowing. The rest of his party did the same.

Chapter 15

The next day Jack took Micheal and Michelle into the castle courtyard to practice their sword techniques

"Hold the sword tight. Don't let your sword fly out of your hand," he said to them, fixing Michelle's grip. "Now swing your sword. Control the sword at all times."

Micheal swung the sword in an even arc but Michelle's sword was unsteady.

"No Michelle," Jack said, correcting her. "You have to let the sword move on its own."

"Like this?" Michelle asked, swinging her sword in another arc that was still off balance.

"No. Micheal show her," Jack said. Micheal repeated the process, followed by Michelle. Micheal's sword was swinging gracefully through the air while Michelle's was shaky and unable to flow.

"UGH," Michelle groaned. "I can't do this."

"Yes you can," Jack said.

"I'm a mage not a swordswoman!" Michelle said angrily.

"Come on Michelle," Micheal said, "It's easy once you get the hang of it."

"You're a boy!" Michelle said. "It's easy for you."

"Jack!" Selena called from behind. She was approaching with the queen and Max. "Let's fight!"

Jack looked at her, struck dumb. "No!" Jack replied as they approached.

"Yes," Selena said. "Now."

"Why?" Jack protested.

"Because I said so."

"That's not a good reason!" Jack kept on protesting.

"It is and you're going to fight me," Selena said. She then drew her sword and charged at Jack.

"Woah!" Jack yelled, hastily drawing his blade and blocking her strike. "Stop!"

Selena swung her blade in an arc, making Jack take a few steps back to protect himself.

"Get ready," Selena called to him. "I'm not going easy on you."

With no other choice, Jack drew his other two swords. He held two swords in his left hand, blades pointed at opposite directions from each other, his right hand holding Hogo. Selena charged at him; his blade aimed at his torso. Jack caught the blade with Hogo, barely blocking the blow. The force of the blow travelled up Jack's arm, making it feel as if he hit his funny bone. Jack swung his left arm in an arc, swiping at Selena with the bottom blade. Selena took a step back, allowing Jack to move his right arm and take a step back.

Selena came at him with a steady stream of stabs. Jack used his left arm to block the attacks, alternating between the top and bottom swords, the clashing of their swords sending sparks flying. Timing her, she was able to stab ninety times in a minute, a feat he had never seen before. The speed of the stabs caused her arm to be a blur and the only way he was able to intercept the attack was because he was using a domain which showed him exactly where the next blow was coming from.

After five minutes- and four hundred and fifty stabs- Selena slowed enough to allow Jack to counterattack with a swift blow. Selena intercepted the blow and took a step back in line with the shock wave so that it didn't affect her. Not many fighters were willing to take this step back and stop pushing forward but this tactic allowed the fighter to gain room for the next attack and dull the blow.

The step back also allowed the opponent to push forward in an attack. Jack didn't miss this opportunity and tried swiping his left arm at Selena. Selena, although she took the step back, swung her sword and hit Jack's arc in mid-air with enough force to send his swords flying.

With the swords gone, Jack gripped Hogo with both hands and brought the sword in a long upward strike aimed at Selena's face. Selena nimbly leapt aside to avoid the attack and stabbed at Jack, his sword still at the height of his arc. With no other choice but to use his secret defensive technique, Jack pulled the sword downwards and intercepted the point with the metal cap at the end of his katana called the tsubaki. The force of the impact caused a ripple starting at the point and moving outwards, blowing Jack's hair and making the grass bend at his feet.

Fear in his eyes, Jack grew desperate, throwing Selena's sword in an upward motion and aiming a kick at her thigh. Selena dodged this and aimed another stab at Jack's throat, stopping before impaling him completely.

Jack lost the fight. Selena pulled her sword away and sheathed it. Jack, breathing heavily, sheathed his Hogo as well.

"You're a boy. It should be easy for you to beat me," Selena said smugly. Jack was looking at the ground but didn't need to look to know that her eyes were on Michelle. Jack smiled at the ground, sweat dripping from his nose as Jack realized Selena just taught Michelle what he couldn't.

"You use three swords," Amaryllis said.

"Yeah, I do," Jack said, still catching his breath. He walked over to his two fallen swords, picking them up and sheathing them.

"I'd like to talk to you, please, Jack." Amaryllis said. "Selena and Max have volunteered to take over for you."

"Umm...sure," Jack said. He turned to Michelle and Micheal, "Work hard you too. I'll check you later."

***

Jack and Amaryllis walked down an open corridor lined with roses on the pillars which overlooked the fields that the Pegasi lived in. The sun was beating down on Jack and it reflected off of the queen's dress and jewels at her throat and on her ears. Her dress was backless to allow freedom of her pale blue wings which glinted like smoky glass in the light. Her pale green skin was visible and her long blue hair waved in the breeze.

"I must tell you Jack, I detest this war," the Queen said, her voice downtrodden.

"I'm sure you do, Your Majesty. I'm sure many other persons share the same sentiment as you do," Jack replied.

"Yes, I agree. But I am a leader. I should be planning a way to prevent this war, not planning an attack," Queen Amaryllis said sadly.

"That's true. But then this was forced on us."

"Do you think peace talks will work?"

"I can't say. After all, I haven't spoken to the demons, and I do not know the intentions of this war," his voice was flat.

"What then do you think I should do, Jack?"

"Can't say. That's your decision."

"You still don't trust me, do you?"

"Can't say you've given me much reason to," Jack said, with zero compassion.

"You're quite confident to speak like that, aren't you," the Queen said.

"Your Majesty, I am an S Class Adventurer who comes from a noble family. There is no one here strong enough to harm me. I wasn't chosen on a whim you know," Jack said.

"I suppose," she said, ending the topic. "Now then, I need to talk to you about our mission."

"Yes?" Jack asked.

"To get to the place the stone is kept, you will be riding Pegasi. But the place it is kept will not allow the Pegasi so I will be sending a guide with you."

"Ok thank you."

"Also, the place used to be heavily guarded."

"Used to?" Jack asked. "As in past tense?"

"Yes. The guards were all removed. A dragon suddenly appeared in the area and killed any who got too close. It was strong enough to protect the stone, along with the enchantment that was in place to guard it so we decided to not interfere."

"I'm sorry but shouldn't your guards have been able to see a dragon coming?"

"Yes, they would have, if the dragon flew or walked there."

"And it didn't?" Jack asked incredulously as the conversation became more absurd by the minute.

"No. It just appeared one day. We believe it was the stone itself that brought it as a guard for itself."

Jack scratched his beard that he had let grow since he got out of the gateway. "Well, I guess that makes sense. The spatial stone would have the power to instantly make a dragon appear."

"Yes exactly," Queen Amaryllis said.

"When can I meet the guide?" Jack asked.

"This evening," Amaryllis said.

"The enchantments, what are they?"

"I am afraid I can't disclose that, Jack. There is a binding vow on my tongue. I am physically unable to say."

"Very well."

***

That evening, Jack returned to the courtyard where Michelle and Micheal were being trained. They had improved vastly under Max and Selena tutelage. Michelle now swung her sword in a perfect arc, able to complete up to four simultaneous slashes without stopping. According to Selena, a man could never teach a woman to use a sword because they were too different. Jack had heard this before, but observing Michelle and Micheal, who looked extremely similar, he could clearly see that they held their feet differently from each other and that their centre of balance was different.

Also present were two women. They were obviously mother and daughter. They both had pale skin, a teal colour and long black hair.

They also shared the same light-coloured eyes, the colour either blue or green, ambiguous in the evening sunset. They were introduced as Chelsea and Lattice.

Chelsea was almost as tall as Michelle and had no wings. Her mother was four foot five and had white wings. Lattice was the current head of the Greenberrie family, which occupied the first seat of the smaller thrones in the throne room.

"So, the woman heads the family?" Selena asked Lattice.

"Yes," Lattice answered. "Women rule over Arthe, after all."

"They do?" Selena asked.

"Yes, they do," Chelsea answered. "Unlike Earth, Arthe is matrilineal."

"Wow," Michelle said. "Earth really should be a lot more like Arthe then. It would be better."

"No, it shouldn't and no it wouldn't," Jack said, cutting her off.

"Do you support oppressing women?" Micheal asked, raising his eyebrows in a judging manner.

Everyone turned to Jack waiting for what he would say next, whether they should all be offended or not.

"Currently, the majority of Earth is democratically controlled. Any hierarchy, either a matriarchy or a patriarchy, will be a step back. Even though this realm has thrived, I do not think we should go back to a centralized power that decided everything on its whim. After all, I could easily say that Arthe should be more like Earth, but that isn't the case. I support neither the matriarchy nor the patriarchy."

Max laughed. Then Chelsea. Then Selena. Then they were all laughing while Jack stood deadly serious looking at them. Max put his arm on Jack's shoulder, catching his breath between laughs. "Jack...my boy," he said, his speech broken by laughter, "you do have a point...but the way you said it...we were all on edge there for a second..." more laughter with tears running down his face, "...for a second...a second, we thought you were a supremacist y'know. You were so serious about it to...like everything you were about to say was God's word."

They all doubled up laughing at Max words, except Jack.

After a few seconds, Chelsea stopped. "I'm sorry," she said, "but did I hear Max call Jack 'my boy'? Isn't he the oldest?"

They all started calming down to answer Chelsea's question, and Selena finally answered. "Jack is the youngest of us."

Chelsea laughed, thinking they were joking. "Really?"

"Yeah," Selena said. "He's twenty-one."

"And the rest of you?" Lattice asked.

"I'm 29," Max said. "And Selena is 28." Selena followed with a nod of affirmation.

"I'm 25," Michelle said.

"Oh ok. What about you?" Chelsea asked, turning to Micheal.

"Michelle and I are twins," Micheal said.

"Oh right," Chelsea said, slapping her face in her hand.

This caused them all to laugh again, including Jack this time.

"I'm 21 to, Jack," Chelsea said, winking at him. They all laughed again.

"Ok ok," Jack finally said. "Chelsea. Fight me."

"Ok," Chelsea said. "Let's get into the open."

"That was easy," Michelle said, giggling.

"I like to fight," Chelsea said. "Plus, after I saw that fight today, I want to fight Jack too. Make him get owned by a woman for the second time today," she finished, winking at Jack.

Selena and Michelled giggled. "Whatever," Jack said. "Nothing wrong with having a woman beat you. But Selena was strong."

The two girls stopped giggling. "You think I'm not strong?" Chelsea asked, fire in her eyes.

"We'll see in a few minutes," Jack replied. He removed his jacket and placed it on the ground, then headed over to an open area in the field. Anger visible on her face, Chelsea followed him. She drew both the swords on her belt and took her stance. They were held in red scabbards and were both shining blue, made of the same material as their daggers, rungrous khiev. Jack unsheathed Hogo, holding it out in front of him.

"You aren't using all three swords?" Cheslea asked furiously.

"No, I'm not," Jack said simply.

"Don't underestimate me!!" she replied more furious than before. "I'm strong. This is a serious fight!"

"Let's begin," Jack said calmly. "Selena, call it."

Selena removed her own jacket and threw it in the air. When it touched the ground, Jack rushed Chelsea with a downward slash using both hands in a move called Absolute Dash, a quick move that involved the user reaching the absolute limit of his speed and closing the gap between him and his opponent as quickly as possible. For Jack, this was 0.2 seconds.

Chelsea barely blinked, but was able to block the attack with both her swords crossing and locking in place. She threw the attack off of her, making Jack stumble back. She then took a few steps back while Jack was regrouping and took another stance. She started spinning her swords and moving them in front of her body in an arc. The blades spin so fast that it was all a blur, and even with all the training and mastery Jack and the others had, they were unable to see the blades. Chelsea didn't stop though, and instead spun faster until the blades looked like one opaque circle with no flashes of light to signify there were two blades.

"Can't see it can you?" Chelsea called out.

"No," Jack admitted simply.

Chelsea laughed, not slowing her blades. "This is my ultimate attack. You can't attack me without getting minced, and if I advance you can't defend."

"I could attack from behind," Jack said.

"You think I would let that happen? I'm far faster than you."

"True. Come then."

Chelsea smirked and ran forward, swords in front of her. Jack stopped the attack. In an instant the blades stopped spinning and were locked in place by Jack's sword. Chelsea was stunned. Jack cupped his left hand into a fist, hitting Chelsea with the back of it and knocking her to the ground.

***

Everyone stood in a circle around Chelsea. She opened her eyes, searching for Jack. "How?" she asked, as soon as she located him. "You couldn't see the attack."

"No, I couldn't," Jack affirmed.

"So how?" Chelsea asked again, her voice loud and angry. "You shouldn't have beaten me!"

"No," Jack agreed. "No, I shouldn't have beaten you. But you see, I was able to break past your technique. And I won."

"But how?" Chelsea asked, louder and angrier than before. Her hands curled into fists and scraped the ground. "No one can break past my technique. It's impossible. No one's eyes are so good!!!"

"No. No one's eyes are so good. But," Jack said, "swordplay isn't only about your eyes. It's about your nose, ears, mouth, soul and body. Everything plays a part in swordplay. Your sword plays a large role too. I never believed this, but three months of sparring with Selena, we fought 16 times and I lost 16 times. After 16 losses, I began to trust my blade and my instincts and I grew stronger. When you learn this, you will see that you can see through any techniques."

Chelsea's eyes filled with tears and she made no move to get up nor speak.

Chapter 16

The next day Jack took Micheal and Michelle in the courtyard and started practicing their parries. Max was also there practicing moves with his dagger. His shirt was off and he was covered with sweat. Curiously, the sweat on the arm holding the dagger was frozen and every time he moved the dagger closer to him, the sweat would freeze on his body and fall off. His breath was also coming out as thin streams of mist.

Jack took a short swing at Michelle, which she blocked with her own sword. Jack raised his sword for another swing and Michelle got ready to parry. Just then, he noticed movement and saw Lattice coming towards them.

"Take a break," Jack said to Michelle and Micheal. He raised a hand as Lattice came closer.

"Jack," she said. "Good morning."

"Good morning, Lady Lattice," Jack replied. Max also stopped his movements and the three of them added their greetings.

"Jack, I need to ask you something," she said.

"Sure," Jack said.

"Ok. When you first came to the castle, you were attacked."

"Yes..."

"You used three swords."

"Yes. I use a three-sword style of my own invention. I used it against Selena too."

"Yes, but you made your swords fly."

"Yes. There are different strategies based on magic use and physical use."

"Ok. But you also flew."

"Yes... a lot of mages learn to fly eventually...."

"Yes, but you were different. You did all this without saying a spell."

Jack looked at her trying not to betray his shock. Disguising it with bravado, he raised his head a little and asked with a smug look, "How do you know I didn't say it under my breath?"

"You didn't," Lattice said, with absolute surety. "And the longer we pretend you didn't, the longer we'll stand here when you should be training them."

Jack considered his position for a second, then held out his arm and extended his fingers. From each finger shot a thin stream of water.

"Wow, you really do perform incarnation less spells," Michelle exclaimed.

"Yeah. I've been doing it since I was a kid," Jack replied.

"How does it work?" Lattice asked. "Could you show me?"

"Me too," Michelle said.

"Same here," Micheal said.

"Ok sure," Jack said. "Hold out your hand and do the same spell I did."

Lattice held up her hand and said the incarnation and performed the spell. Seeing Lattice perform the spell and realizing Jack wasn't expecting an incarnation-less spell, Michelle and Micheal did the same.

"Ok now hold it and memorize the feeling," Jack said. "Once you get it you can stop."

After a few seconds, Lattice stopped, Michelle next and then Micheal.

"Ok now repeat the same thing but without the incarnation."

They held out their hands again then tried repeating the spell. After several moments, Michelle and Lattice did it. Micheal was still unable to do it.

"Close your eyes and focus," Jack said. "Block out all noise, block out everything and focus on the outcome."

Several moments passed with Micheal's eyes closed and finally he was able to produce a weak stream of water from his fingertips that ended after two seconds.

"Good," Jack said. "It took me around a year to get it right but I was doing it on my own."

"You mean you figured it out on your own," Lattice said. "I'm sure someone else would have taught you."

"Yes, I'm sure that someone else was able to do it," Jack said. "But the concept behind it is pretty complicated and to consistently use it is pretty hard. I learnt it on my own though."

"Explain," Lattice said.

"Well, first you have to understand mana. There are three types, Observation Mana which you use on your senses for techniques like Mana vision and Mana sense, Physical Mana, which you use to coat blades, your arms and use raw to create weapons of mana like the Phantom Sword technique. Finally, there is Elemental Mana, which converts raw mana of armament into elements like fire, water, etc.

"Next, you have to understand the form. There are basic invocations of mana, such as when you run mana through swords to strengthen them, but then there are techniques that give shape to mana to control their behaviour. Mana Scope of observation mana acts like a telescope, Phantom Sword which takes raw Physical Mana and shapes it into a sword which is able to slash the surroundings, or Spiral Flames, an Elemental Mana technique that creates a tornado like blast of fire that charms enemies.

"By being able to distinguish these different mana types, and by being able to call up and shape the mana, you can form spells without speaking."

"But how does this actually work?" Michelle asked, still confused. "The spells are vital to any technique."

"Not true," Max interjected, before Jack could respond. "Swordsmen, gunners and many close combat fighters learn to focus the mana into their bodies to boost their physicality. Sonic Dash and Absolute Dash are examples, where fighters focus all the mana into their legs to boost speed."

"True," Jack affirmed. "Also, spells don't really mean anything-"

"Woah woah woah," Micheal interrupted. "Did you just say spells don't mean anything?"

"I did. And they don't."

"Unbelievable."

"Listen please," Jack said coldly. "Spells progress with the mage. If spells were definite, the instant you use a spell it should make something happen, and if it is definite, it would draw out as much mana as needed or available in the caster."

"That's because the spells only do what the caster wants," Micheal defended. "The power level is determined by the caster. If he inputs a certain amount, the spell will respond to that."

"Let's try an experiment then," Jack said.

"Ok," Micheal responded suspiciously.

"Spells can be said in any language. I'll show you the outcome of the spell and then I'll give you the Japanese incantation and you repeat it," Jack explained. He then held out his hand and made dust stream out of it. "The incarnation is, 'Mume ni shimaikonda mama no.'"

"Ok, here goes," Micheal said, holding out his hand. "Mume ni shimaikonda mama no." A stream of dust formed and shot out of his hand.

"Nice work," Jack said. "That spell was a fake. It's a line from 'Beautiful' by the band Treasure. It means 'It's still stowed away.'"

"What!?" Micheal shouted incredulously.

"Yup. Spells are subconscious. They exist to prompt the user. You know what else exists to prompt the use? Ninjutsu. Japanese hand signs used by Ninjas to perform spells. They do nothing but help the user to perform the spells easier."

"So-so...." Micheal stammered.

"So, the spell doesn't matter. All that matters is the caster's ability to perform a spell."

"So why doesn't everyone use it more often?" Lattice asked. "As far as I know, only elves and dwarves have ever been able to do that."

"Well, I'm not sure about Elves and Dwarves, but it took me a year to master casting a spell. It took me another ten years to be able to consistently use spells in battle. And that's the ones I learnt. If a new spell is presented to me, I won't be able to perform it in an instance like I do with the others."

"I see," Michelle said. "So, the only reason you were able to do it was because of years of practice."

"Exactly," Jack said.

"What's your arsenal of spells like?" Max asked.

"I know fourteen different spells," Jack replied. "That's fourteen basic spells with variations of each spell."

"I see," Lattice said. "Thanks."

Jack nodded. "By the way, Max, how come you didn't try it?"

Max looked at him seriously for a second then turned away from him. He took a few steps away from them, then raised his dagger. The blade glowed for a second and Max brought it down in an arc, cutting the air with a blue stripe. From this stripe, icicles formed with deadly points and fired off. "I can only do it with ice spells," Max said. "It comes as naturally as sword fighting for you. It's muscle memory."

"Wow," Jack said, amazed. "Actually...yeah, that's a nice way of putting it, muscle memory. "

"Yeah," Max said, smiling at Jack.

"Thanks for the lesson boys," Lattice said to Jack and Max. "Also, I already asked Selena, but Jack, will you and Max join me for dinner tonight?"

"Oh," Max said, surprised.

Jack looked over at Micheal and Michelle, noting that they weren't invited. Knowing he couldn't reject it without being rude though, he replied, "We would be glad to."

"Good. I'll see you both tonight," Lattice said, turning and walking away.

Max and Jack looked at each other but didn't say anything since they didn't want to hurt Micheal and Michelle's feelings.

***

The Queen provided Jack, Selena and Max with clothes for the evening. Jack and Max were dressed in clothes similar to the Spanish Navy during the 1800s, Jack in red and Max in blue. The tassels on their shoulders, the buttons and the lining were all gold. Selena was in a blue open backed dress which clung to her body. Jack was sure that it was made for a fairy since it seemed tight for Selena. Jack's clothes were tight and he had no doubt Max was suffocating as he was by far the largest of their group.

Lattice served meat and vegetables unknown to Jack but the meat was similar to deer meat. The flesh was red and chewy and between bites Jack, Selena, Max, Lattice and the other guests were speaking. Present at the dinner table was Lattice's husband who was named Bennidect, Chelsea and Chelsea's younger sister, Andretatch, Dre for short.

"So, you introduced yourself by your first name?" Jack asked Lattice in the middle of dinner.

"That is correct," Lattice said. "Most nobles would introduce themselves by their last name as is customary, but being called by my family name is so off-putting."

"I like the name Greenberrie though," Selena said. "It's easy to say."

"I quite agree," Max said.

"You also introduced yourself by your first name," Chelsea pointed out. "And you're all human nobles."

"Quite right," Max said. "But I never really got with the whole 'noble-person mentality.'"

"And Jack and I don't use our name. No one knows my name and Jack goes by Drake," added Selena.

"What do you mean by 'noble-person mentality'?" Dre asked, leaning close to Max. She had the same teal coloured skin as her mother, but her eye color was different; a sparkling blue.

"Well..." Max began, realizing what he said next could be offensive with present company, "I am a fighter. I often sleep on forest floors and in crevices of caves. I never really roamed a castle or wore anything other than armour."

Chelsea and Dre laughed. "Nice save," Dre said, flashing a smile at Max. Max looked slightly relieved to not offend anyone.

"So," Bennedict inquired slowly, his voice soft and raspy, "Why don't you both use your noble names?"

"Well..." Selena began.

"It's easier to blend in if we don't carry our noble names," Jack butted in, saving Selena from having to explain. "We're both warriors so it's easier to interact with non-warriors if we looked and acted like them."

"Yeah exactly," Selena said.

Lattice nodded and smiled. Chelsea spoke up, "Quite right. I also do the same when I'm on duty. Instead of 'Greenberrie' I am 'Kin.'"

"On duty?" Selena asked.

"That's right," Lattice replied proudly. "My daughter is the commander of a legion in the Queen's Royal Army."

The conversation about rank and an explanation about the Queen's army carried for most of the dinner. Following this, they asked about Earth technology and the advancements humans made. When finished eating, Chelsea, Dre and Bennedict excused themselves from the table, leaving Selena, Max and Jack alone with Lattice.

"So, Jack," Lattice said when Chelsea, the last of the three, left. "You may have noticed that I did not invite Micheal and Michelle to our dinner." Lattice had finished eating and so were the others. This was purely an audience disguised as a gathering and Jack knew whatever she said would be extremely important.

"Yes, I picked up on that little detail," Jack replied. Lattice's gaze was fixed on Jack and Jack looked directly into her eyes. Max and Selena were silent, observing the two.

"Don't you think I'm rude for not inviting them?"

"It's your house and your dinner table. Whoever comes is up to you." Lattice smiled. "Smart boy, that response. Very diplomatic. Actually, I wanted to talk to you about them."

"Sure," Jack answered suspiciously, not sure what was coming next.

"They're twins, am I right?"

"Yes, you are."

"And they're different genders?"

"They are."

"At first they looked identical. I was unsure whether they were boys or girls on first meeting them."

"Twins usually look similar."

"No. Not when a boy and girl are born at the same time."

"What are you getting at?"

"There is a rare mutation, not in humans, that causes twin elves to be born with different genders and be exactly similar."

"Micheal and Michelle are both human."

"Are you sure?"

"Yes."

"How can you be sure?"

"Because..." Jack began slowly. "They look like humans. Elves have pointy ears."

"True. But if they're hybrids they would look like humans. Elves and human are extremely alike, but for the ears."

"If they're hybrid elves that is their concern."

"It is."

"So then why the concern?"

"Because elves aren't the only race with that mutation. Of course, the other race is very different and they'd have characteristics of that race which would be noticed immediately."

"They're definitely human," Jack replied defensively, decisively.

"But how can you be absolutely sure?"

"They performed human only spells," Selena interjected, speaking for the first time since this conversation began.

"They did?"

"Yes, they did," Jack said remembering. "There is a specific spell only humans are able to use and it's impossible for elves to perform."

"Very well," Lattice conceded. "They're not elves."

"Yes, well we should get going," Jack said, making an excuse to leave. He wanted to get as far away from Lattice as possible.

Chapter 17

Two days after the dinner, Jack and his team were ready to leave. The Queen herself saw them off. Bennedict was present but Lattice did not make an appearance. Seven Pegasi took off into the air, the seventh carrying food and clothing for the trip.

They soared over the treetops to the west. Looking below them, the Tech Pised housed a manor fallen to ruin. The lower branches held few shops and homes. The manor would have been quite impressive in its younger days, with glass roofs and red brick walls. In Jack's opinion, the manor was more beautiful than the Queen's Castle. But the fields were overgrown and only a few stray Pegasi grazed there. There were vines growing on the walls and as Jack passed overhead, he saw several panes of glass missing from the roof and windows.

They cleared the area and flew over the forest. He spotted several settlements as they flew further west. Below on the ground, utilizing Mana Vision, Jack was able to differentiate animals that were indigenous to this realm. Up here, the wind was chilly and the air sweeter than anything he had experienced on Earth. Jack closed his eyes and let his Pegasus take him along.

"We'll set down on that cliff," Chelsea yelled over the wind.

Jack opened his eyes and saw that the forest had ended and they had entered rocky grounds with a mountain looming infront them. "Ok," Jack yelled back.

***

The Pegasi landed as gracefully as ever. The grass on this cliff was knee high and green. It overlooked a valley where there were several rocks. Jack walked to the edge and looked out.

"This cliff is the last place the Pegasi can feed for the rest of the journey to the Stone," Chelsea said from behind. "There's a spring here that keeps the grass watered. You can all fill your bottles there to. After here the sun won't reach us so cherish it while it's here."

"What do you mean the sun won't reach us?" Michelle asked.

"We're going into that valley down there," Chelsea replied.

"Oh ok," Selena said. "You're not scared, are you?" she teased Michelle.

"No, I'm not!" Michelle replied.

"Let's get something to eat," Chelsea said. "That Valley is your final destination."

"Does it have a name?" Max asked.

"Sunstone Valley. The stones at the top of the valley collect sunlight. The stones are gathered from here and used as fertilizers for the trees the material of your clothes came from. It's crushed into a fine powder and introduced into the water supply. The dragon that appeared here discouraged anyone coming close though and the valley filled up with rocks."

"Interesting," Micheal said. "Does the stone have magical properties?"

"Not that I know of. You can go check though."

"After we eat," Michelle told them.

"They used to allow people to just go look for them?" Jack asked.

"Before the dragon appeared, the area was heavily patrolled by guards and regulated. There were also some animals but since the dragon appeared the merchants stopped coming and most animals have fled. There are some demi-humans down there that befriended the dragon as well."

Jack pondered these words as the group gathered preparing for a meal. They lit a fire using magic and Michelle put food to heat up in a skillet. There was a meat similar to the one they ate at Lattice's house and vegetables. There was also bread and a golden liquid that Jack was sure was Nectar or a similar drink.

When food had been served, Micheal asked Chelsea, "How come you don't have wings?"

Chelsea paused with a bit of food in her mouth. Michelle nudged him for asking such a blatant question.

"Well..." Chelsea said hesitantly. "It's because I'm a hybrid."

"You are?" Max said, looking up.

"I am."

"What races?" Micheal asked, Michelle nudging him again.

"Don't ask questions like that," she told him.

"It's ok," Chelsea said. "I'm half-human."

"That's so cool," Micheal said, his sister scowling at him.

"It is?" Chelsea asked.

"Yeah, it is," Micheal said. "You don't think so?"

"Not exactly. I'm a noble but since I'm half human I don't get the same treatment as others. I can't sit on the throne nor can I lead this country. It's also where I get the human name Chelsea instead of something more fairy-ish. Plus, my teal colour will fade in time."

"That's horrible," Selena said.

"It is. The nobility part and skin part, not the name part," Micheal said. Silence followed this, no one knowing what to say.

"Well, I'm glad you guys don't judge me," Chelsea said finally

"Of course not," Micheal said. "Hybrids are pretty cool, you know."

"How do you know?" Selena asked.

"Hybrids trained with us," Michelle replied. "We were pretty close to them."

"Wow, that's so cool," Chelsea said.

"Yeah it was," Micheal said.

Silence followed this for a while, broken once again by Chelsea. "So Max. How does it feel to be an alpha-human?"

Max looked up from his cups surprised since he had remained quiet since then. "Well...I believe it's the same as everyone else."

"It is?" Selena asked.

"It is," Max replied.

"But you have an innate compound ability. How is it the same?" Micheal contributed.

"Well..." Max said. "It's true that we are born with the ability to use a compound nature. But we aren't born with the knowledge so we do have to master it. A compound ability doesn't matter if you can't use it."

"That's true," Michelle said. "I guess it's not really an advantage when you realize you still need to train and master the ability."

"Yeah," Max said. "Actually...overall...I believe it to be a disadvantage instead of an advantage."

"A disadvantage?" Chelsea asked, shocked.

"Yeah. My family focuses on Ice Spells but doesn't really focus on the other elements. Well apart from water and wind."

"Well..." Michelle said, "that's just natural right?"

"Yeah, I guess it is," Max said.

After their meal, Micheal, Michelle, Max and Selena went looking for sunstones in the valley, leaving Jack and Chelsea alone with the Pegasi.

"So, Chelsea," Jack began, having stayed quiet throughout the meal, "what happened to the manor on the West Tech Pised?"

Chelsea, who was lying on her back in the grass, raised up a little and looked at him. "Well it's quite an interesting story."

"Tell me," Jack said, looking into her eye, which he now saw was green.

"The original occupants of the manor are the Silvaene family. They were once nobles in the Queen's court. But they conspired against the queen and they were all killed in an attempted coup. The remainder of the family, who were not present, were tried and ordered to death or banished. Their property and assets were siezed and the place abandoned."

"Oh wow. And the queen really fought them off?"

"No she didn't," Chelsea said solemnly.

"What do you mean?" Jack asked, confused.

"The queen they attacked was the current queen's mother. She died in the attack. Queen Sindervelt took over after that at the age of seventeen."

"Oh wow. She was so young."

"To take the role of queen, yes. But there's no such thing as too young or too old to lose your parents."

Jack looked at her, noting that her voice sounded reminiscent.

"The throne they had was also removed, leaving a total of six smaller seats and six advisors to the queen. My mother currently holds the second and my sister will succeed her eventually."

"I see," Jack said. "And no one tried getting the property or influencing the queen to make them a seventh noble?"

"No. The queen left it as a reminder to the people. It is believed that one day the Silvaene family will come back and fall back into favour with the queen or the next queen to be."

"I see. I wish them luck then." Jack lay down next to Chelsea with his hands behind his head.

"Are you jealous of your sister?"

"What?"

"You sounded jealous for a second."

"I was born a hybrid but I'm the oldest. I'm supposed to get the throne but since my dad was human, I can't get it."

"So, you are jealous?"

"No. It's not her fault, and thrones are overrated. I do miss my dad though."

"I see. I miss my dad too."

"What happened to your dad?"

"He was a knight. He died in battle."

"I'm sorry to hear."

"Thanks. I barely saw him though. He died when I was young and before then he was often away doing knight stuff."

"Oh, I see. I never met my dad. He died before I was born and I never got to see him. He did name me though."

"At least you have his name," Jack said, looking on the bright side.

"Over dinner you said you weren't a knight. What are you?"

"I'm an adventurer, same as the others. We don't follow any kind of military rule, we just do our own thing."

"But why not? Wouldn't it be better for you to be a knight?"

"My brother is a knight. I'd say we're the same."

"He followed your dad's footsteps?"

"Yes. I come from a family of powerful mages and knights. They were the best of the best."

"And you?"

"Me?"

"Yeah."

"Well, when your family is the best at everything, there isn;t much for me to do. So, I just live my life how I want."

"So, why'd you take the mission?"

"Because, if there was no Earth I can't live how I want."

"So, you're doing all this because you feel like doing it?"

"I'm also getting paid."

"Well...that is something."

"Yup."

"And if you didn't feel like doing it?"

"You'd probably be talking to my brother right now."

"Ah I see."

"Guys, they have no magical properties," Micheal called, heading towards them from the Valley by a little road way. "They's just some nice rocks."

"Here. I brought you guys some," Selena said, following Micheal.

Chapter 18

Chelsea led them into the valley by Pegasi for some way. After a while, they set down and started walking. The valley was too narrow for the Pegasi to fly, a feature that directly contributed to this location being chosen since it would make it harder for anyone to get to the stone.

"Keep your eyes peeled," Chelsea said, her voice echoing off the walls of the Valley. "The dragon scared away most people but the toughest. They should allow us to pass but if they don't it'll be a fierce battle."

Jack put his hand on his sword ready to fight at a moment's notice. Their walk through the valley was uneventful for the most part. They had to jump over rocks that were wet with condensation. In a few places they saw some pools of water. The light from above refracted downwards off of the condensed water on the walls of the valley, causing the valley to sparkle. Jack noticed several small caves along the walls and wondered if anyone lived there.

Selena came up behind Jack and nudged his elbows. Jack looked over at her, directly into her eyes for a moment. Jack nodded to her to show that he understood. They didn't need to say a word but they both knew the same thing. Selena sped up, overtaking Jack

Jack stooped and picked up a pebble which he skipped along the track and bounced it on Max's shoe. Max turned his head slightly and raised his eyebrows at Jack to show he understood. Selena walked up behind Chelsea and walked alongside her, their hands brushing for a moment. Micheal and Michelle were walking behind them. Jack turned around for a second and called to them, "Don't lag behind you two."

"We won't," Micheal called back.

They apparently didn't realize what was happening. Jack pretended to trip on a rock. He stopped for a second and concentrated on reading the mana pretending to get up. He couldn't sense anything through the mana. He was sure though and Max and Selena confirmed it.

They were being watched.

Max and Selena were calm and collected. Chelsea was a bit more tense. Jack made his body relax and move naturally to ensure that their observers didn't realize they knew they were being observed.

They walked on for another kilometre or so until they arrived in a circular area with no rocks. Chelsea walked into the circle followed by Max and Selena. They were now visibly tense. Selena's fingers twitched ready to draw her sabre for an oncoming attack. Max looked around at the walls. Jack stopped and allowed Micheal and Michelle to walk in front of him. He followed them, his left hand on the hilt of his sword ready to draw.

An arrow flew directly at Micheal. Jack nearly missed it. If he was in front Micheal would have been hit. Jack rushed forward and swiped the arrow out of the air. More arrows flew from all sides. Max and Selena drew their weapons deflecting arrows. Chelsea drew hers a second later, spinning her swords to create a barrier. They formed a circle around Micheal and Michelle who weren't expecting an attack.

Micheal raised his staff and conjured a tornado above their heads silently. The arrows were drawn into the whirlwind and crushed. Max pulled out his dagger and plunged it into the ground. From the point of the dagger everything was covered in a thin layer of ice. Jack was covered till his knees in a thin layer and so were the others. Looking over at Max, Jack saw that the hand holding the dagger and the whole left side of his face was covered in ice, as were both shoes. He opened his mouth and his breath came out as a little cloud.

Jack kicked out his legs and broke the ice covering it. He then jumped up on a ledge that was above them, ready for any attack that should come. Instead, he saw that there was a now frozen crossbow that was seemingly operated from a distance.

Jack checked the other places where arrows were fired from. He found more frozen crossbows here. Jack jumped down, landing back into the circle.

"The arrows contained no mana," he heard Michelle say.

"We couldn't sense them," Micheal said.

"They were operated from a distance," Jack said, walking towards them. "There were eight crossbows, repeaters. All that was needed was a way to pull the trigger. There wasn't anyone to infuse mana in them."

"I see," Michelle said. Her voice sounded frightened. "Do you think they were left over from the army that was stationed here?"

"No. We're being observed," Selena said.

"That's enough," Jack said. "Be careful. Let's move. Standing here and talking won't help us."

"He's right," Chelsea said. "Whoever attacked isn't here. We should move."

"Max, can you move?" Micheal asked. "Half of your body is covered in ice."

Max moved and broke off the ice attached to him. "Yeah, I'm fine."

Jack nodded at him and motioned for Chelsea to lead the way. They started walking again, on high alert, the ice crunching beneath their feet. Their weapons were all drawn and Micheal and Michelle had their staff ready, the sun and moon raised to start casting a spell. They walked in front, ready to deflect anything that came towards them.

"Jack," Selena said. "That area was clear of rocks. If those crossbows were left by the army, the rocks would have fallen and covered it."

"I know," Jack replied in a low voice. "Whoever they are doesn't want us to find the Spatial Stone."

"How do you figure?" Selena asked. "What if they want to steal it?"

"Who would want to steal it?" Max asked from behind.

"Demons," Selena said.

"Demons? How would they get here?" Max asked her.

"They could have used the Gateway."

"They would have been intercepted at the major gateway."

"True. But if they used the Human-Fairy Pathway they wouldn't have been seen. In fact, we practically cleared the way on this side."

"No," Jack said. "Whoever it was doesn't want us to get the stone. If they wanted to steal it from us, they wouldn't have ambushed us and made their presence known. And if they wanted to kill us and take it themselves, they would have killed us with spells from above."

Selena looked at him and was about to reply but didn't have a chance.

"We're here," Chelsea called from in front.

The party approached a cave. It was double Max's height. In the inside of the cave Jack could see a structure fallen into ruin which he figured guards would have lived in. There was another smaller structure that was flattened and burned. This must have been what had happened when the dragon appeared. Some weapons heads were strewn around the place and a couple scratches and burns on the walls which evidenced a fight. Everything else was moved away.

As they walked deeper in, something shot out of the cave heading to them. Chelsea intercepted the attack since she was in front of them. A large figure covered in armour and wearing a helmet locked swords with her, pushing her back. From behind, two more figures shot out, their cat ears poking out and their tails waving behind them. Selena intercepted one with her sabre and Jack the other with his sword. Max attempted to plunge his dagger into the ground again but was stopped by an arrow aimed at his hand.

Michelle yelled something from behind and the figure locked on Chelsea was blown backwards, the gust of wind blowing Jack's hair from behind. Micheal followed up by throwing the attacker from Selena. Selena then came behind and slashed at Jack's attacker's legs, making him fall over. Max headed in the direction that the arrow was shot from.

He slashed his dagger into the air, firing off a number of projectiles at a fleeing attacker. Jack ran after Max hoping to intercept the attacker. The ran outside of the cave, blinded by a sudden light. A magically conjured light spell, Jack realized.

Coming back inside the cave, Jack saw that his four comrades were locked in combat. The three attackers had gotten up and began a fierce assault. Chelsea was fighting the man with the helmet, while Selena fought the two feline persons that attacked her and Jack. Micheal and Michelle couldn't fire a spell without hitting Selena or Chelsea, so rapid and chaotic were their movements.

Rushing past him, Max charged straight at one of Selena's opponents, his short sword coming in a downward arc.

Jack rushed to help Chelsea. Helmet was giving her a hard time since she couldn't build up enough speed for her usual attacks. Jack rushed in, swiping his sword at Helmet's chest, tearing open his coat. Helmet took a step back. Chelsea took a few steps forward, closing the gap and slashing at Helmet's arm. Helmet dropped his sword and turned to retreat. Jack dashed forward and slammed the butt of his sword into Helmet's helmet, cracking it down the centre and knocking him unconscious.

Turning, he saw that Selena and Max were finished fighting. Max's opponent was covered in ice, his sword broken in the middle, Max himself covered in a thin layer of ice up to his elbows. Selena's opponent was on the ground unconscious and bleeding from some small cuts.

"What now?" Selena asked.

"Leave them," Jack said. "Let's go."

"But-" Michelle began.

"No buts. Do you want reinforcements to come? One of them escaped," Jack said.

"We're already here," a voice from behind said.

Jack turned his sword at the ready. "Put it down," the same person said, an old man with a staff. He was surrounded by ten larger persons, armed with swords and spears ready to fight.

"Who are you?" Jack asked, his sword still at the ready.

"I am the leader of the Felidae, the cat people," the old man said. "My name is Sanict."

"Well, Sanict, you can leave or die," Jack said.

"I think not," Sanict said.

"You think not? Why don't we show you what we think," Jack replied, raising his sword ready for an attack.

"Now now, boy," Sanict said. "Put your weapons down. We only want to talk."

"About what?" Jack asked.

"The Spatial Stone," Sanict said.

Jack's sword wavered. He looked over at Selena, whose sword was also pointed at them. "Very well," Jack said, "I'll listen to what you have to say. You have five minutes."

"Ok," Sanict said, "But let us take our injured."

Jack motioned his approval, and three of the Felidae stepped forward.

Chapter 19

The Felidae let Jack and his party go with few words. They walked deeper into the cave, swords drawn, prepared for a dragon attack. The further inside they went, they observed an increasing number of stalactites and stalagmites. Soon they came to a fork in the road, just as the Felidae told them they would. They would have to find out what was along both of these on their own as the Felidae would not tell them what was beyond here.

"Chelsea, you take Micheal and Michelle along the right path. Selena, Max and I will go along the left. There shouldn't be any more forks so you should be able to stick together," Jack ordered. "If you see the dragon do not engage unless necessary. Come back in twenty minutes or before if you get to the end. Wait here for five minutes and if you don't see us, come in, we might need assistance."

"But Jack," Chelsea said. "Shouldn't you take a mage with you?"

"That's not necessary," Jack said. "Max, Selena and I are able to fight a dragon together and so are Micheal and Michelle. These groups are better."

"You're sure?" Chelsea asked.

"I am," Jack replied. "Also, this is not your mission. You can turn back now and not go forward. You don't need to risk your life."

"No, I'm good," Chelsea replied quickly. "When else will I see another dragon?"

"Are you sure?" Jack asked her.

"I am," Chelsea said.

"Very well then," Jack said. "I wish you all luck."

Micheal and Michelle nodded at him and Chelsea smiled. They turned and walked into the cave; Michelle's staff held high to produce light.

He turned to Selena and Max. "Ready?" he asked. They both nodded. "Let's go then."

He led the way into the cave. There were many stalagmites and stalactites that they had to dodge around, as well as some pillars that blocked their way. They walked further into the cave, water dripping around them. The cave grew steadily darker but they didn't cast any illumination spells or light any fires that would warn the dragon of their presence. They moved on instinct alone, carefully feeling out anywhere they would hit their heads. Jack and Selena had sheathed their swords earlier and drawn their daggers as it would be hard to fight in here with longer weapons. Max had his machete out which was shorter than his shortsword, stained red from his mana, one side a deeper red than the other.

Soon, after a few minutes of walking, they saw light ahead. They walked faster now, as with the light they could see the outline of the obstacles ahead. The pathway opened into a giant cavity at the back of the cave. The cavity had little crystals illuminating the area from the ceiling and walls as well as a large hole at the top that sunlight flooded through. Selena grabbed Jack's arm and pointed downwards.

Looking up at the ceiling, he had failed to notice that there was almost a ten-foot drop ahead of him. One step and he would have died. On the floor were five or six baby dragons piled on top of each other asleep. They had bright green scales like snakes, tiny and almost smooth. They were as large as a full-grown man, their claws tiny.

Suddenly, the words Sanict said came back to him.

***

"What's your name, warrior?" Sanict asked Jack.

"Jack."

"And the rest of you?" Sanict asked.

"Chelsea."

"Max."

"Selena."

"Micheal."

"Michelle."

"I see," Sanict said. "And I take it you are the leader, Master Jack?"

"I am," Jack replied.

"Well then, Master Jack," he began, "I have two things for you."

"Yes?" Jack asked.

"The first is information of the cave. The second is a request."

"I'm listening," Jack said.

"Firstly, the cave. A few meters into the cave, you will encounter a fork in the road. I will not tell you what is at the end of which fork, but at what end there is a treasure, and the other the Dragon you are expecting."

"So we just have to guess the correct one?" Jack asked.

"No," Sanict replied. "Actually, I implore you to go down both, as one holds the key to the other."

Jack looked at him and said nothing.

"Right, well, about my request. I am asking you, when you go into the path of the dragon, do not kill it."

"Impossible," Selena said.

Jack held up his hand and stopped her.

"Sanict," Jack said. "I don't care what reasons you have for wanting to keep this dragon alive. But if it threatens my team, I will not hesitate to kill it. Understood?"

"I do," Sanict said.

"If you want to stop us, now is your chance. We will gladly fight you ourselves," Jack finished.

"That will not be necessary, Master Jack," Sanict said. "I am confident you will come to the same conclusion as I, when you see what is on the other side."

***

Jack heard a loud rumbling and a crash. The cave shook once and stopped.

"What was that?" Max asked worriedly.

"I'm not sure," Jack said. "But let's go find the others." He turned to go back down the path but Selena stopped him. "What?" he asked.

She pointed to the far side of the cave, and another tremor was felt. "A path, leading to the direction they went," Selena said.

Jack considered for a moment. "We'll go that way, but be careful. Move quickly and don't awaken the babies."

Selena leapt down first, followed by Jack and Max. They took off at a sprint, heading for the opening. Selena went in first and Jack followed her. The path was strangely clear of any stalagmites and stalactites. They ran for around a minute and felt more tremors.

They ran out into a cavity slightly larger than the one they had come from. There were crystals here as well as some glowing flowers. The flowers were being trampled by the massive dragon that stood in their way and some were on fire.

The massive dragon was locked in combat with Micheal, who was firing fireballs at the dragons. The dragon blocked them with one wing. The intensity of Micheal's spell was increasing.

Jack had one thought in his mind. He couldn't let the dragon die. Maybe it was Sanict's words. But he was sure it had more to do with seeing the baby dragons.

Jack rushed forward and drew his sword, and turning his blade to the blunt side, he coated it in mana and slashed downwards, sending a stream of mana down at the dragon's neck, knocking it down. Its wing dropped, and Micheal fired another fireball at the dragon. The heat of the blast knocked Jack backwards and singed his hair. The dragon took a step back and roared loudly.

"DON'T KILL IT!!!" Jack yelled.

Micheal looked at him, noticing him for the first time. Jack was scared. There was pure anger in his eyes. A wave of ice covered the ground and the dragon, as well as Jack. The fires that were burning the flowers stopped.

Selena ran up behind Jack and charged the dragon. She raised her fist and hit the dragon on the head, knocking it unconscious. It fell with a resounding crash as two tons of dragon fell on its side.

Micheal raised his staff again but Jack stopped him. "The fight is over," he said, holding Micheal's arm.

Micheal looked him in the eye. He struggled to get free and yelled out, "I'll kill it. I'll kill it like it killed my sister."

Jack was shocked, a chill running through his body. Michelle was dead. He held on to Jack as he realized she was gone.

Chapter 20

After calming Micheal down, Jack told him about the babies in the other room.

"I don't care!" Micheal said.

"Killing it won't bring your sister back," Jack said.

"Like you would care. It wasn't your sister," Micheal shot back.

Selena stepped in. "Where's Chelsea?"

"Over there. The dragon threw her over there. I went to check her out and that's when it attacked us. Michelle stepped in and got slashed. Her body is also over there."

"Come on," Max told Jack. The two walked over to see where Chelsea and Michelle were.

Michelle was lying in a pool of blood, her eyes staring up at the ceiling with a long slash over her entire torso, a deep red colour.

Chelsea was further along, unconscious and on her side. His sword was lying a little distance away. If she had fallen on it, she would have died.

"What were they doing here? The exit is that way," Jack asked Micheal.

"When we came through the pathway, the dragon swiped at her and threw her here. We rushed over to check her out," Micheal said, coming up behind them.

Selena stepped around Michelle and went to check on Chelsea. "She's breathing."

"Good," Jack said. He went up to Michelle, his feet stepping into the blood. He kneeled down and closed her eyelids. "Sorry Michelle. Thank you for your help. I will always remember you."

Selena and Max stood in silence and Jack said a prayer over her body.

Jack took off his jacket and placed it on her body, covering her face.

He stood up and faced the other three. "We have to find the stone quickly and get them out of here."

"It's over there," Micheal said, pointing to a lake. "At the bottom. I can sense it."

Jack looked at him. "Ok. Stay here in case Chelsea wakes up. Selena, Max and I will go in."

"Jack, can I kill the dragon?"

"No. It's asleep."

"If it wakes up?"

"It won't wake up. I'm sure of it," Selena said.

"If it does..." Micheal said.

Jack pondered this. He knew Micheal wanted to kill the dragon badly but he also knew that there were baby dragons on the other side of the cave. He decided to trust in Selena's words and then gave an answer. "If the dragon wakes up, and you have no other choice, kill it. Don't do anything if it leaves you alone and if you can avoid killing it avoid it. You are also not allowed to disturb it while it's sleeping or cause any disturbances."

Micheal chewed his bottom lip. "Fine."

Jack looked at him once more, wondering what Micheal would do. Then he walked to the edge of the lake and looked within. The water was extremely clear but he couldn't see the bottom. He took a breath and dived in. Selena followed, then Micheal.

***

Immediately as the entered the water they were spit out.

"What happened?" Jack asked.

He looked around the cave. He saw Max and Selena next to him. They both got up and looked at Jack.

"Where's the dragon? And Micheal?" Max asked.

"I don't know," Jack answered.

"Listen, Sindevelt said that there was some kind of protection in this place, but she couldn't say what. Be careful ok."

"Yeah." "No problems."

Jack got up and drew Hogo. "I can sense the stone this way. Come on."

"Ok let's go," Max said, drawing his shortsword in one hand and his dagger in the other.

"Yeah," Selena said, drawing her sabre.

They started walking slowly back towards the path with the baby dragons. Instead of entering a cavern with a nest, they instead found a set of golden double doors over eight feet high and ornately designed.

"What is this?" Selena asked.

"I don't know," Jack answered. "But the stone is in there."

"Don't have a choice then, do we," Max said grimly.

"No, no we don't," Jack said. "Help me open it."

He put his hand on the door. Something immensely powerful was on the other side.

"Let's get this over with," Jack said.

"Yeah, ok."

Jack and Max pushed. The doors led to a throne room. Above the throne was an altar, where the spatial stone was placed. On the throne sat a knight in black armour.

"Jack."

"Come on." Jack drew Hogo and stepped into the throne room. Immediately torches on the wall flared to life.

The knight raised his head and its eyes glowed to life.

"Oh no."

The doors slammed shut behind them, trapping them inside with the knight.

Jack drew his other two swords and let them hang in the air, ready to be deployed.

The knight stood up and grabbed his sword from next to the throne.

"Jack that throne is made of bones."

"I can see that. Get ready."

Suddenly from behind the throne several other knights appeared and rushed them.

"Max!" Jack yelled.

Max dropped to his knees and sank his dagger into the floor, instantly freezing the area.

Jack stepped in front of Max and intercepted a knight that was headed towards him. Selena caught one and pushed him back. Three more rushed them. Jack pushed off the one that he had engaged. Max sprang up from behind Jack, plunging his dagger into the knight, freezing him from inside out.

Jack dashed forward and intercepted the three knights headed towards them. He dodged the first and second one and intercepted the third in a blade lock. The two knights who he'd rushed past turned to slash him from behind, but Jack's two tool steel swords he'd left suspended in the air flew to the knights and stabbed them in the back. Selena came running to help Jack but at the same time the Black knight moved. Jack's swords were all occupied. Selena was mid-strike and completely open to attack.

The Black Knight's sword came slashing downward to Selena when Max was suddenly there, intercepting Sword to Machete.

Selena's sword came crashing down, slicing off the head of the Knight Jack was engaged with while Max held the Black Knight in place.

Jack moved away as soon as he felt the knight's sword lighten and moved around Max and Selena to slash at the Black Knight.

The Black Knight jumped backwards the full length of the throne room, out of Jack's reach. He raised his hand and more minion knights came rushing out.

Jack made a movement with his hand. His two tool steel swords rushed out of the bodies they'd impaled and rushed to his side.

"Both of you get behind me," Jack said.

Max and Selena both got behind Jack, ready for what came next. Jack moved his hand in a circle and the swords started spinning extremely fast.

"Wait."

The Black Knight jumped off his throne and rushed towards the trio behind his minions.

Jack slashed his hand downwards and both of his swords shot forward, decapitating the knights as the came forward. The black knight moved out of the way.

"Wait."

The Black Knight rushed them and Jack made a sign with his hands, calling the swords back to them.

The Black Knight was in Jack's face. He slashed his sword at Jack who intercepted it with Hogo.

"Wait." Jack's voice strained as he held up the Black Knight's sword with his own.

Jack flipped Hogo up and pushed the Black Knight's sword back. The Black Knight slashed quickly though, and Jack could just barely block it. His tool steel swords suddenly came hurtling back, completing the cycle Jack had set and cut off one of the Black Knight's arms.

"Now."

Max and Selena shot out like springs under intense pressure towards the Black Knight. Selena aimed to cut of the Black Knight's other arm, while Max stabbed at his head, hoping to freeze him from the inside out.

The Black Knight's other arm fell with a thud, but he jumped backwards before he could be stabbed.

The Knight landed on his throne and his arms grew back a second later.

"This isn't going to work," Max said.

"I realized. Gimme a second to think of something," Jack said grimly.

Chapter 21

"Listen, you two hold back the knights. I'm going to fly up and get the stone. As soon as I get it Max get those doors open and let's go."

"Ok." "Yes."

The Black Knight raised his hand and more minion knights rushed out. Jack focused his mana and blasted off from the ground, aiming for the altar suspended in the air. He landed with a thud on the floor. There was a black mensa in the centre with a purple stone sitting on a golden podium. Jack walked forward.

Jack could sense the battle raging behind him. He needed to get the stone and get out of here before anyone got hurt.

Suddenly the Black Knight was behind him. He swiped at Jack, who jumped back. The tip of the blade cut into Jack's chest as he flew back.

Jack raised his sword in front of him, ready for the fight. The Black Knight rushed him, so fast that Jack could barely block. Jack parried the blade and swiped at him, hoping to weaken him. His cut wasn't serious but it was stinging. He hoped the Black Knight's sword wasn't poisoned.

The Black Knight slashed at Jack's head. Once again, Jack wasn't fast enough to dodge and he got slashed on the face above his left eye. Blood splattered his vision, nearly blinding him. He couldn't sustain a drawn-out battle.

He closed his eyes, focusing on sensing the Knight through the mana only. He collected his mana on the blade of his sword and swiped at the Black Knight, letting loose a rush of mana that cut everything in its path.

Jack took a breath and stopped the bleeding. He then focused himself and pumped the blood through his body faster, raising his body temperature incredibly high. He rushed the black knight, trying to cut him. The black knight dodged out of the way of Jack's sword.

Jack dropped to his knees and slammed his palm on the ground. He let loose a shockwave of wind that caused the altar to shake. He then caused a mini tornado to spring forth where the Black Knight was standing, causing him to jump away.

The black Knight raised his sword and slammed it down on Jack's stooped form. Jack raised Hogo, blocking the attack but struggling to hold back the blade. The Black Knight pressed the sword onto Jack, close enough for Jack to see his reflection.

Jack pushed back, spinning his sword in a way that the Black Knight was thrown off.

Jack sprang to his feet and created a dust bullet, commanding it to curve and forcing the Black Knight into a corner.

Then he opened his hand and the blood on him collected in a ball in the palm of his hand. He formed his blood into a dense ball and shot it at the Black Knight. It pierced his armour and entered into his body. Jack commanded his blood to disperse in the knight body, and then ignite. The Black Knight burst into pink flames from the inside out.

Jack was panting. His wounds stung. "Move," Jack said to himself.

Jack stood upturned his back to the knight and plucked the stone. It was extremely light and there wasn't anything remarkable about it. It looked like a glowing piece of amethyst, about two inches in diameter.

"You're way too much trouble. You made me use my trump card."

Jack rushed out of the altar and looked down.

Max and Selena were surrounded by bodies, looking up at the altar and waiting on Max.

"Guys I got it. Let's go." Max raised his fist in victory and then rushed to the door and opened it.

Jack landed next to them. "At least it's not locked."

"What happened to the Black Knight?" Selena asked worriedly

"I killed him."

"You're hurt," Max said.

"Yeah, don't worry. We have medical supplied outside. Let's go."

Chapter 22

"Can I see it?" Micheal asked as they emerged from the water.

"Me first," Max said.

Jack shrugged his shoulders and passed it to Max. "He helped get it."

Max inspected the stone. It was translucent and smooth in an oval shape. It was also pretty powerful. He could feel the mana of the stone and the warmth it exuded. One of the most powerful objects in the universe and it fits in his palm.

He held it out and Selena took it. "Hey!" Micheal called.

Selena stuck her tongue out at him, another piercing showing. "What does the council want this for anyways?"

"I don't know. Maybe it can restore the Gates."

"Ah. That makes sense," she said. "Here."

She passed the stone to Micheal who held it up to the light to inspect it. "Truly magnificent," he said, then put it in his pocket.

"Woah there, champ," Jack said. "I'll be keeping the stone."

"No, you won't," Micheal said, turning away from them. "Actually, you're going back to the human world empty-handed."

"What?" Jack asked, getting up. "What are you talking about?"

"We're bringing the stone to the Demon King," a voice called. Jack turned his head at the sound and saw Michelle looking perfectly fine.

"Michelle!" Max called. "You're alive." He got up and started in her direction.

Jack raised his arm to stop him. "What is this?" he asked, his voice colder than any spell Max could cast.

"It's simple," Micheal said. "You're all staying here while we head over to the neutral territory and give this to our king."

"Your king?" Selena asked.

"Yes. You see, we're half-demon."

"Half-. Lattice was right. You are hybrids, but who would have thought you were demon hybrids," Jack said.

"No, no one suspected. Not even our mother knows. We figured it out on our own. Our dad was a demon, a noble actually."

"So, you're doing this for your dad?" Selena called.

"Yes," Michelle replied simply.

"What about your mom?" Max asked.

"What about her? She's dead," Micheal returned.

"And you faked your death," Jack said, gritting his teeth. He didn't want an answer, he just needed to say it.

"Illusion magic," Michelle replied anyway. "Comes in handy."

"Where's Chelsea?" Max asked.

"Asleep," Micheal said.

"Enough of this," Jack said. He charged them and drew his sword. Micheal raised his staff and fired a gust of wind to push him back.

"One spell. I learnt one silent spell for this," Micheal said. "Thanks for showing me by the way."

Jack gritted his teeth. Selena rushed past him, heading for Michelle. She was using Sonic Dash to boost her speed. Michelle aimed a fireball at her, but Selena disappeared from in front of her and appeared behind instead, slashing at her back. Michelle blocked the blow with the centre of her staff, but it was still cut in half under Selena's blade.

Max plunged his dagger into the ground, freezing it from the point outwards. Jack drew his other two swords and hurled them in the air at Micheal.

Michelle raised the bottom section of her staff and slashed it in the air, cutting it with a black ribbon. Selena fell to the ground when it touched her. Michelle stepped away from her.

Micheal plunged his staff into the ground, sending a shockwave of dark magic from the point, blasting away the ice.

"You're not the only one with a special innate ability," Micheal said. "We're half demons. We can use dark magic and we both have dark stones."

Jack's swords came around for an attack from behind directed at Micheal. Micheal blasted these away with the same wind spell. His swords stuck on to a nearby rock unable to get free.

"Get Micheal," Jack said to Max. He then used Absolute Dash to attack Michelle who threw up a barrier of Dark Magic. "You saved my life!" Jack shouted at her.

"I needed the stone," Michelle shot back, but he could see something else in her eyes.

Jack's sword flew out of his hand. He was pushed back by the force of the barrier, hitting a rock.

Max raised his dagger and from the point a stream of pure ice magic shot out at Micheal. Micheal raised the base of his staff and a raw stream of dark magic shot at Max. The two beams collided, blue and black fighting for supremacy.

Ripping the stone from around his neck, he gripped it tightly in his hand, shooting a stream of raw, unchained, unrestrained wind magic at Michelle. Michelle raised her section of staff and shot the same dark magic stream as her brother. The green and black fought for supremacy over each other.

The air grew colder as Max's spell took the advantage. Micheal was more skilled, but when it came to raw power, Max had the advantage. The lake behind him froze and ice was spreading along his body as his spell grew more intense. Knowing he would lose, Micheal decreased the power of his spell for a moment, then released it in an explosive force that threw Max backwards onto the frozen lake.

The force of the spell caused Jack and Michelle to stop their spells. Michelle shot a quick ball of darkness at Jack which he managed to dodge. The resulting explosion threw him sideways.

Micheal made his way towards Michelle and put his hand on her shoulder. "Farewell Jack," Michelle said, swiping her broken staff at the roof. Stalactites and crystals fell and showered down on them. Grabbing his sword, Jack rushed to block any falling rocks from hitting Selena.

"Chelsea," Jack shouted.

Max got up and headed over to her location drawing his machete to prevent her from getting hit.

Jack got one last look at them as Micheal fired a spell at the roof of the passage causing the entrance to crumble.

Epilogue

After returning to the human world, Jack was confined to his home. Selena and Max were sent to their families. They were all awaiting a hearing to discuss why they failed and what action would be taken.

Jack was practicing his three-sword style in the garden. His left eye was bandaged where he got cut fighting the Black Knight. Luckily there were no poisons. He saw Shanks approaching.

"I'm looking for your brother," Shanks called.

"He's upstairs," Jack replied without stopping his motions.

"I heard about your failure," Shanks said.

This caused Jack to stop. "And?"

"No one expects a team mate to betray them."

"And?"

"And it's not your fault."

"I'll cut you."

Shanks smiled at him. "What are you going to do now?"

"I'm supposed to wait for my hearing."

"And?"

"That's all."

"So you're just going to wait?"

"That's what I was told to do."

"Hmm...ok then. I'm going to find your brother."

Jack watched him go. What did Shanks mean? Shouldn't he do what he was told?

He pondered this well into the night. Then he came to a decision. He was going to find Max and Selena, then they were going to the neutral ground to confront their teammates.